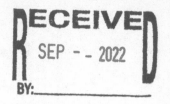

D1007351

Prepare Her

Prepare Her

Stories

Genevieve Plunkett

Catapult
New York

ISBN: 978-1-64622-040-3

Cover design by Nicole Caputo
Book design by Wah-Ming Chang

Library of Congress Control Number: 2020943101

Catapult
1140 Broadway, Suite 704
New York, NY 10001

Printed in the United States of America
1 3 5 7 9 10 8 6 4 2

For Steven Bach (1938–2009), who encouraged me to "continue writing—anything and everything."

Contents

Prepare Her

Something for a Young Woman

◆

1.

The shop owner, by then, knew all about it: the girl's hatred of elbows and stray pieces of hair; how her boyfriend disliked the taste of her lip gloss; how she referred to far too many body parts as "it." He knew which details she had made up to appear more experienced, even what she had swept over in an attempt to be coy. He listened to her, as bosses do, with hands folded, waiting through her blushes and her flights of qualifiers. The corners of his mouth and eyes remained still.

The girl and the shop owner liked to talk. Once, they had been talking in the storage room, searching a heap of bubble wrap for a lost piece to a tea set, and he had gotten very close to her, blocking the door with his body. She had looked up and met the buttons of his shirt, tugging across his torso, and a flight of nerves had gone up inside her, like someone had smacked a screen door covered in moths. He had joked that someone might walk in and get the wrong impression, as if life could just be so funny.

It had come to this, surely, by the girl's own indiscretion—not just her candidness, but some kind of postural lingering, something learned but unconscious. She started to spend more time in front of the full-length mirror on the inside of her closet door, so that she could see all the way to her heels, which she raised off the floor. She saw less and less of her boyfriend, and when they spoke she thought she detected something in his voice, like the hook of suspicion. They broke up two months later, although it had nothing to do with the shop owner.

"If I were to ask you what your preferences are," the boyfriend asked, "what would you tell me?"

The girl told him that he needed to be more specific.

"Your preferences," he said again. It was an odd word for him to be using, she thought, but before she could answer, he continued, "Well, mine are different. People already know."

When she went to work the next day, the shop owner was there, feeding the woodstove. She told him about the breakup and their strange conversation and he turned his face to the fire, to hide from her, she imagined, whatever satisfaction he could not, for the moment, subdue.

"I was wondering when you were going to find out," he said.

He stayed for the day, when he would have usually left her in charge, and chopped firewood behind the building, hauling armload after armload inside with his sleeves rolled up past his elbows. It was the sight of the sleeves like that—the meat of his forearms darkened by hair—that made her wonder if something had changed between them and if, perhaps, he was waiting for her to do something about it.

There was a large desk where she sat, in the back, by the stove. On one side of it, there was a stack of old magazines, and on the other, a shallow wooden box of loose postcards, mostly photos of old bridges and the fronts of hotels. The middle of the desk was kept clear for the exchange of money, the sliding over of small purchases in folded paper bags. She didn't know what put it in her head to sit there—some adolescent notion of sexual liberty—but she knew, the instant that he returned and saw her like that, that it was the wrong thing to do.

The shop owner dropped his eyes to the side and waited for her to climb down, then handed her the keys and told her to lock up in thirty minutes. She watched him go and heard the triple clatter of the bell above the door. There would be no more shoppers at this time. People did not like to stop roadside after dark, especially not to lurk through the twilight of scuffed velvet and sad lampshades. Still, she waited until closing time. She took the money from the cash register and recorded the profit onto a slip of paper. The drawer, now balanced for the next morning, was locked into the register, and the envelope of cash was placed in a small safe beneath the desk.

The next week, the shop owner said that he would be on vacation with his family and, since the girl would be off from school, it was up to her to look after the shop. He assured her, in his instructions, that there would be enough chopped wood for the fire until he returned. She wondered, briefly, how she must have appeared, on top of the desk like that. She knew better than to worry that he would speak of it, but she also knew that it would always exist, as a small loss on her part.

She worked diligently while he was away, even though she was alone and could have easily spent the time reading books or using the phone. She even dusted the stuffed emu that had remained unsold for so long that it had acquired a name, chosen by the girl who worked there before her, who had occasionally been mentioned by the owner with unwavering neutrality.

At the end of the day, she locked herself in to count the register. Because the shop owner was not there to collect it, the money began to pile up in the safe. Then one night, the girl unlocked the safe to find the money gone, replaced by a small brown box. For a moment she feared that they had been robbed overnight, but then she saw that the box had her name written across the top.

Allison.

Inside, under a sheet of crepe paper, was a necklace with an oval black stone.

Formal. Something for a young woman.

2.

Allison met the man that would become her husband during their last year of college, then followed him to the city. He was always saying that he had friends there. She didn't know why she was surprised when the friends did, in fact, exist, all together in little compartments over the street. Like the college boyfriend, the friends had been biology students, but they spent a lot of time playing guitars plugged into big amplifiers, which they once accused her of moving two inches to the right based on dust patterns. There had been shouting. The college boyfriend had flown to her aid, his ears turning pink with outrage. She had cried and cried from the commotion. The city was making her sick with its fumes, its pockets of hot breath and burnt rubber. She swore that the cupboards smelled like newborn mice.

"I have this thing where I can't be around vomit," the boyfriend had said the first time it happened and put up his hands.

It was the pregnancy that caused them to move back north, to be closer to his family. His parents owned a large property with a barn, but you couldn't call it a farm; the horses were old, likely to trot back from the pasture favoring a hoof, and the chickens were slowly disappearing. There was speculation of a fox, as if such a creature in that area needed speculation.

Their decision to get married seemed not to rely on whether it was the right choice but rather on if his relatives in Canada could make it to the wedding, and if it was better to try to hide the belly or wait until after the baby was born.

"Things usually go back to normal," said the woman who would be her mother-in-law. "Before the third one, at least. And by the fourth, you don't care, just as long as it isn't another boy."

Theirs was a boy. They named him after Allison's late grandfather. He was born in January, in their own undecorated living room, with the rug rolled up, so that it would not be stained. It was how the baby's father had been born, same as his brothers, all four of them. Ideal, maybe, in the old family homestead, with its hearth and its lambskin throws. But this was a one-story ranch, spare of furniture and not fully unpacked. The midwife had needed a pan to collect the placenta and they found one in a cardboard box, next to an unwrapped sushi kit and a ceramic cat with hearts for eyes. Come on, Mama, the midwife had said throughout the labor. Come on, like someone coaxing a stubborn cow.

By summer, they were married on his parents' property, under a rented arbor. These decisions—the birth, the wedding—as well as others, were made with the earnestness of dogs wanting to be good. They painted the nursery yellow, because that was the color of the husband's room when he was a boy. She could not dispute this logic, she knew, without weakening the mortar that had fixed together happiness and bumblebee yellow always in his mind. Even though, the way she saw it, bumblebees were mostly black.

In college, she had played the viola. She had always imagined herself in the symphony, with her straight, narrow back, wearing something thin, dark, and almost glittering. In the city, that may have been possible, but so far north, and now with the child, there were only opportunities in the early and late summer, when there were weddings.

Her husband's cousin played the cello and knew a wealthy couple who had taken up the violin years ago, as an answer to their "echoing empty nest." They formed a quartet and met at the cousin's church, in the basement, playing "Jesu, Joy of Man's Desiring" between spines of stacked folding chairs.

The night before their first performance, she found herself struggling to find something to wear. Something around her middle had changed since the baby, who was now four months old, and there was a veiny tint beneath her eyes. She found the necklace with the black stone in the back of a drawer, still in the box with the crepe paper, and put it on for the first time. The shop owner had never spoken of it, and she had never felt an obligation to wear it for his sake. She had taken it in the way someone might receive a confession: not entirely certain whether power had been granted or taken away. Still, the weight of the stone flat against her skin brought the small pleasure of knowing that she was once something unknown to the people there, to her son and to her husband.

The boy grew, healthy and cheerful, and often satisfied to play alone. Allison took advantage of this, retreating to her room to work through a bit of complicated fingering. Sometimes, talking to the boy, discussing what color spoon he should use, or whether or not it was a good idea to dip his teddy bear into the bath, left her voice feeling frail, caught in the pitch of adult-to-child deception. Something needed to be purged, and so she would work it through the instrument, following an earthy, resonant phrase, like walking a trusted path.

She worked, too. The husband brought in only so much as a high school science teacher, which had him in fits at the end of the day. Why, he wanted to know, was there always some teenager trying to tell him that whales were not animals?

"They probably just mean to say that they are not fish," she suggested, even though she knew it would make his eyes clench in mock pain; his fight was wearying, the enemy ever more insidious.

It was her husband who got her the tutoring position at the high school's library, which was better than her last job behind the counter at the coffee shop: being looked up and down by the worldly, latte-drinking citizens, scanned by their eyes for general intelligence, sex appeal, usefulness; being asked, in so many ways, what had gone wrong in her life. But even with her pupils,

she was always up against a sneer, another dirty attitude, waiting for her to slip up.

Her in-laws took the child during this time, which
she was grateful for, even though it depressed her to
hear them ask, every day, Are you a good boy?, and to
hear them say, Watch your footing, be careful, until the
anxiety was too much for him and he fell. That and they
wanted to put him on a horse, which she fought outright, until they wore her down. It was an old horse,
they said, a slow horse. Her husband had ridden it when
he was a boy. All the boys had.

They saddled the horse on the first warm day in
April. The saddle was a western-style, large enough that
mother and child could both sit without being crowded
by the horn. Her mother-in-law would ride ahead on
her pony and their horse would follow. There was nothing to worry about.

The husband's family owned acres, stretching into
the forest behind the house, but it was no use riding
where there weren't any paths, so they followed the
neighboring fields. As long as they stayed next to the
tree line, where they would not trample the crops, it
was fine. Allison felt her shoulders relax. If she closed

her eyes, she could feel down through the trunk of the animal beneath her, down to the planting of each giant hoof.

"A tractor," said the boy, as they rounded a line of trees. He was excited to see a piece of machinery, like a familiar face in the wilderness. It was parked at the far tree line, by a woodpile. Allison could make out the form of a man, carrying out a repeated swaying motion with his body. As they approached, it was clear that the man was taking wood from the pile and throwing it into the back of a four-wheeler. Every time a log would crash into the bed, the sound would bounce off the side of the tractor, doubling up in echo.

As they passed, the man threw in another log with a crash, causing the mother-in-law's pony to bounce in annoyance, firing a little blast from under her tail. In response, the horse Allison was riding buckled at the knees, then danced from side to side before leaping forward at a full gallop. The reins fell from her hands, the boy shifted to the side, and at the same time she had all the time in the world to think of what to do. There was no hope of stopping. She kicked off her stirrups, hugged the boy to her chest, and let herself roll off the side of the saddle so that she would hit the ground with her back, her body a cushion for his. It was so very easy to maneuver. She felt like she could laugh.

When she hit the ground, the air burst from her lungs. And she had a clear sense of déjà vu, accompanied by a thought: This is where it happens. It has always been right here. It was as if she and the boy had taken the fall over and over again, recycled throughout eternity.

Her breath returned. The child struggled to free himself from her arms so he could watch the big horse thunder back to the barn, kicking up bits of horseshoe-shaped mud along the way. He was unharmed, unconcerned even. No one, for that matter, seemed alarmed. The mother-in-law, in pursuit of the runaway horse, could be heard whooping its name from the next field over. The man at the woodpile, who'd seen the fall, did not slow his swinging arms, nor did he call off his dog when it went to investigate the two figures on the ground. The dog licked the boy with a wet muzzle, pushing its insistent face back into them, no matter how Allison held out her arm.

Her in-laws did not call it an accident. Neither did her husband. There was a lesson to be learned for the boy.

"He'll have to get back on sooner than later," said the father-in-law. "We wouldn't want him to develop a fear."

But that was just what Allison wanted: to arrive at the edge of a cliff and to back away, preferably on hands and knees; to see a rabid animal and to barricade the doors, call the fire department.

They told her that she was worrying too much. The runaway horse had been found after the incident, standing square in his stall, eyes half closed. Just a big marshmallow, they said. A teddy bear. We'll just put the boy on his back, while the horse grazes in the field. As if that were somehow safer.

They lifted him by the armpits, red-faced and kicking, onto the back of the horse, who chewed, drooling gobs of green saliva.

"There," said the in-laws, with some breathlessness. "Now he can get down."

Allison watched the boy run back into the house; then she sat on an overturned feed tub by the pasture fence. She wondered why everything was wrong, why she couldn't just be thankful that everyone was alive, that bombs were not falling from the sky.

3.

A year later, she found herself separating from her husband. There had not been an affair, or even an argument; it was just that he had left for a long weekend to attend a job training and she had not wanted him to come back. It was the anticipation of his face, drawn in fatigue and pained by private failures; the dirty swill of his eyes scanning the kitchen, the living room, looking to see what had changed while he was gone, or what still had not been done.

The training was for science teachers, kindergarten through twelfth grade. It was held somewhere in the Adirondacks, at a state park, in a small concrete building filled with beaver pelts, animal scat references, and cicada casings. The teachers slept in cabins and took cold showers in the outbuildings in their flip-flops.

"We learned how to dissect owl pellets today," the husband said over the phone. "You know what they are, right? Tell me what you think they are."

She had been about to throw a basket of laundry into the washing machine but set it down, standing over its armpit smells, the acrid shadow of his pillowcase that she'd washed twice already since he'd left. She sighed.

"It's all the mouse parts that the owl can't swallow."

"Well," he said, the word drawn in, a dumpling at the back of his throat. "The point is that you didn't say owl poop, which is what half the people here said. Half. Can you believe it?"

"No." She gave the basket a nudge and it slid almost the entire way down the basement stairs, hissing, like skis, before it flipped and bounced to the bottom. She knew that the stain on his pillowcase wasn't really a stain, just the place where his head ground into the pillow at night, the one place in the house that would always smell most like him and would always remind her of a thumbprint in cheese.

He was upset to hear that she wanted to leave, but not as upset as she thought he would be. He told her to take the child and move to her hometown, only two hours away by car. He was certain that she would want to come back after some time alone. He would send her money. He would tell his parents that she was going to spend time with a sick family member, so that they would not think poorly of her. Everything would be fine. By the time they were finished discussing it, she was not entirely sure that the separation had not, in fact, been his plan all along.

◆

Her parents' house still had the aluminum swing set in the backyard from when she was a girl, with the same slide, always dappled by the repetition of rain and soil. Their rooms were made up for them, complete with towels laid out on the bed, like a hotel. The boy was adored. Her decision was never questioned.

She found work at the elementary school, taking over temporarily for a music teacher who was having a baby. There was a lot of cardboard and glitter and toilet paper tubes, stopped at the ends and filled with beans for shaking. There was no epiphany, no rush of dark pleasure now that she was on her own; just "I'm a Little Teapot" during the day and dinners at home of macaroni and cheese with little cubes of hot dog.

When she first took out the viola, it sounded dry from the travel. Her mind would drift; her bowing arm would become heavy. There were certain steps to be taken, she knew, for moving on, like chopping her hair, doing something drastic, but not too ugly. Her mother urged her to meet people, to "build a foundation," but she would not; she was comfortable, for the time, living in a blind spot, off the grid of where she had pictured her life heading.

And then one day, in February, a change occurred, marked by a dream. It was one of those dreams where very little happens, but something is injected under the surface, into the commotion of life, drugged by sleep. When she woke, she remained in bed for some time, seeing his face in the rumpled darkness, while falling snow and ice hissed against her window.

In the morning, she was still stirred, but with an added dint of sadness. Her husband had called her the night before, the way he did every Sunday, to ask about the boy and to inquire, nervously, about her plans. He told her that he hadn't felt like seeing anyone else, meaning women, and then waited a long time for her to respond. He talked about his students. He wanted to know if she had heard that narwhals were in fact mythical. Did she know that brown cows can only make chocolate milk?

She focused on the slight breakage at the end of his questions, the great effort he put into pronunciation that could only be described as "toothy." She had tried to imagine that this would be the last time that they would ever speak, even though she knew he would call again next week. She had imagined what it would be like to see his traits emerge in the boy as he grew, traits that she may or may not have taken for granted in the past. But there had been only weightless, drifting apathy, like the fatigue from artificial light.

She went outside to clear the snow from her car and then work on the layer of ice on the windshield wipers. You could sometimes forget that there was something to be uncovered once you got to chipping and scraping, as if the point were to just keep working until you hit the ground. Exhausted, she opened the car door and sat, freezing, behind the wheel. She looked at the gray sky, the corroded white of birch trees, through the hole of visibility that she had cleared on her windshield.

In her dream, the shop owner had been sitting behind the desk by the open stove, the same large desk that had been there when she worked for him, years ago. He was writing in some kind of financial log with his sleeves rolled up and his arms glowing in the light from the burning coals. He would not look at her. He would not speak to her.

She turned the key in the ignition and was blasted by cold air. Inside the house, she knew that her mother would be making coffee, while the boy ate his cereal in the kitchen, scrutinizing the cardboard box (why he could never put that kind of concentration into a real book, she would never know). If she left now, they might not even notice that she was gone.

By the time the hot air kicked in, she had already taken the exit off the highway and pulled into the gas station across the road from the old antique shop. She would wait for ten minutes, she told herself, and if she did not see the shop owner by then, then she would go home, call in sick to work, and come right back. She would sit there in her car all day if that was what it took.

She prepared herself to wait, but when she raised her eyes, he was already there—just a shadow behind the window of a pickup truck, rolling to a stop in the gravel parking lot in front of the shop. The man emerged, hulking in a gray overcoat, and walked to the shop door, where he kicked loose an icicle on the gutter. Her first impression was, not surprisingly, that he looked older—he had been in his fifties when she worked for him, almost ten years ago—but he still had the same broad carriage, the same security of strength. She could see his beard, now fully gray and trimmed close to his jaw. The rest of his face was hidden beneath the furred brim of his hat. She watched him unlock the door to the shop and disappear behind it, imagined him switching on the overhead lights and then going straight to the woodstove. Something knocked around inside her chest, half-winged and terrible.

She went about the rest of the day distracted, unable to focus on her regular tasks, as though she were still in that frozen car, peering through the narrow hole of cleared ice and snow. At school, she unlocked the storage closet and dragged out the xylophones and frayed squares of carpet for her students. She let the time pass in the clumsy gallop of misplaced mallets and little voices off-key. When the last school bell rang, she drove home, stopping by the neighbor's house on the way to pick up the boy, who had been there since lunch. She must have strapped him in the car seat, she must have put his mittens over his hands, for although she didn't remember doing so, he was there, dressed and asleep, by the time she pulled into the gas station again. The antique shop across the road did not close until six and it was not yet four, so there would be little chance of seeing him. Still, she sat, warming the tips of her fingers in the heating vents, just in case she caught a glimpse of shadow, some small sign that he was inside. That was all that she needed.

Half an hour passed. From where she was parked, she could see the items on display in the window—an iron-ribbed trunk, a stenciled child's sled, a mirror reflecting the purpling clouds overhead—and behind them, a sliver of depth, the only suggestion of the space beyond. So far, nothing had crossed it, even though her eyes had remained fixed, pooling with concentration. When the child woke, he wanted to know where they were. He was hungry and cold. Allison turned on the radio, she dug through her purse for a candy, but the boy only began to cry. Defeated and annoyed, she drove home, determined to return to the spot in the morning.

But the next morning, she felt differently. With horror, she recalled the events of the day before and found each moment distorted by something that she now felt no connection to. Toward the man, the shop owner, for whom she'd waited so long to see cross behind the window, she felt only disgust. She would never go near the place again.

Weeks passed and the strangeness of the day had not returned. A freak reaction, she told herself, caused by stress, or the long winter. She developed a better practice schedule and, through regular use, her viola regained its familiar give, as if ripened. When she played, she dipped into something that was always streaming, moving like ants through the veins of a colony. There, she was all feelers, little bits of armor, a million tiny, uncrushable hearts. They poured from her instrument and found their way in swarms through the cracks in the walls, slipping outside beneath the skin of the trees, down into the earth, where the egoless are.

And then, on a day in March, she woke before sunrise and could not fall back to sleep. Her mother's little dog was up, dancing its toenails against the kitchen floor, so she put on her jacket and clipped the leash to its collar. Outside, it was unseasonably warm. Her muscles relaxed and her mind wandered. She wished that she had someone to call other than her husband, whose conversation was still irritatingly stoic.

"We lost another chicken at the farm," he would say. "Maybe you will have an answer for me by spring."

She had tried to speak to her husband about the incident with the horse after it had happened, about how time had slowed and she had maneuvered her body to protect their son. About how she had felt that it had all happened before. This is where it happens.

"Adrenaline," had been his response. "An amazing thing."

But that wasn't what she had wanted to talk about. She knew the mechanics of it as much as anyone. What she wanted was for him to ask her about something ridiculous, like her past lives, or if she ever flew in her dreams and, if so, whether she flapped her arms or kicked her feet. She wanted him to ask her about the people in her life who'd hurt her and for him to be surprised at her answer, impressed by the depth of her life before him. It wasn't about revealing her soul—a word that she wasn't sure if people were still using seriously, like Pluto—but about giving the tangential a place in their life, casually but also mindfully, just as one might start putting a feeder out for birds in the winter.

She let the dog put its weight into the leash, as if she could get away with following it, across town, to where the houses had shapelier gardens and names on the knockers, to the street where the shop owner lived with his wife. The windows of the house were thick with sleep, with gray-blue deafness.

She took a seat on the curb directly across the street from the slope of his front yard, where the crocuses were already coming up along the lattice under the porch, little wet paintbrushes of purple and yellow. The dog sat obediently and looked with her, working its nose against the wind. There was no bench, no view, no reason to be there. She should not have been there, but she waited as the cars came with their headlights spreading over the road and as birds dropped down and picked over the new ground. She waited for the light to turn on, and when it did, downstairs—a little yellow heart, beginning again—she stood up and walked back.

When she returned to her mother's house, the boy had just risen and was looking for her with a watery, worried stare. He wanted her to pick him up, up, up, as if to break through the atmosphere.

4.

That fall, she wore the black necklace to the shop owner's funeral. When she read his name in the obituaries, it did not register immediately. Was that really how it was spelled? Was that how it looked on paper? Because it was not how it felt, spun into malleable lint inside her mind. She wanted to know if it was him or just someone with his name.

She was shocked to see the open casket—as if it were something that he had consented to—and it shook her opinion of him, just a little. She considered reminding her husband, who still called every Sunday night, that she wanted to be cremated, but then wondered if that knowledge would somehow tie her permanently to him, "until death."

She remembered, as a child, dreading the body of her grandfather, her son's namesake—not because of its appearance, but because she feared that she would be expected to say something to it, a prayer that she had not been taught. Her six-year-old cousin, the only other child attending the wake, had huddled by the fireplace, shivering. I'm cold, he told the grownups, I'm too cold, and they shook their heads. You can't take that kid anywhere, they had said. He's always hogging all the attention.

Years later, during some unremarkable moment—sitting in school, or riding in the car with her feet on the dashboard—it had suddenly occurred to her that her cousin had been afraid of the body but did not want to admit it. What a terrible world, she had thought, and she still felt, from time to time, that a boy, who was probably scolded for saying things like "cross my heart and hope to die," was expected to see a corpse and act accordingly. Stepping into the funeral home, she vowed silently to save the children, should there be any inside.

There was one, a little girl wearing a purple jumper over a black turtleneck, who swung her legs from a tall armchair while reading a paperback. She did not appear to need saving. Allison stood in a line to the casket. One moment, she was looking at the spider veins at the hemline of the skirt in front of her, and the next, she was over his face. Some nearby vent was pumping cool air, which, although odorless, she wanted desperately to avoid, like the puff of wind from under a train. The face before her looked pained, as if caught in the state of being about to swallow. A poorly executed clay figure; a creased sock at the bottom of the laundry basket. She felt the pressure to move along, so that someone who actually knew him could gaze, move their lips.

And then she was in front of the man's wife, not realizing that she had entered another line. The wife had an open expression, a face of recognition, perhaps left over from the person who had been in front of her just before. The skin around her eyes was gluey, caked-over red.

"Oh, Allison," she was saying. "Allison, Allison, Allison. Look how you've grown up. Thank you for coming."

The line moved on. Conversation trickled as people

willed themselves into circles, trying to place their connection to each other, like stringing beads.

"Do you know how it happened?" It was the girl in the purple jumper, leaning back in the chair, her arms spread wide in ownership.

"No," said Allison. "Do you?"

"My mom said that his heart kicked it, but I don't believe her because my dad looked at her weird when she said it."

"You're not afraid to be here?"

"Grandpa looks like the trees when they talk in cartoons," said the girl, swaying dreamily. "They talk and then their faces just go back to looking like bark. That's what I say." She curled back the front half of her book and forced a sigh.

Allison walked home with her hands plunged into the pockets of her cardigan, digging into the give of the wool. She waited for a weight to lift, or to descend, some indication that her life was affected by the man's death, but felt only the pain of her shoes where they rubbed, up and down. It was a Friday afternoon, still two more days until her husband would call, leaving openings in his speech, places where she knew she could lay out her decision and have it met tactfully and with absolution. She stopped to look up at the glint of a passing jet, which had been roaring inconspicuously through her head for some time. How lucky I am, she thought, watching the plane blink into the clouds, to still have someone waiting for me to make up my mind.

Arla Had Horses

◆

In school, they were taught to use the phrase "I know someone who."

"Don't think of it as tattling," Mrs. LaFlamme told them and she began to lower herself onto the floor. In order to sit on the carpet the way the students did, that is, Indian style, she had to lift one of her legs and place it with her hands over the other. This action inspired a childish wobble, in which she seemed to be testing her buttocks, to find which one would best support her. On Fridays, she wore light-colored jeans with elastic bands around the ankles, which reminded Renee of the denim scrunchie that her mother had twisted over her ponytail that morning, the scrunchie that was supposed to balance out her outfit, also denim. On picture day, Renee's mother had insisted that she wear a dark green jumper to match the wallpaper in the downstairs hall, where the photo would be inevitably framed and hung. She had a plan, she had said, for the next seven years, and she spread her arms, indicating all the empty space on the wall. Renee's mother had plans for a lot of things.

"Don't use those scissors," she'd say. "I have a plan for them."

Her mother liked things to be a certain way, which could also mean that certain details, such as the particular wash of denim in her daughter's outfit, or the weight and thickness of curtains, had a direct effect on her mood. She was "not a dog person." Of this, she was the most vocal. Dogs, according to her, "were just undirected energy." And so Renee was allowed to have a turtle, because the turtle was in possession of a brain that was much more to the point. Renee was not so sure of this, but she did appreciate the way that the turtle maneuvered a bit of lettuce into its mouth—purposely, like a sock puppet trying to eat a sandwich.

"I know someone who smokes a pipe when he walks his dog," said a boy named Carter.

"I know someone who smells like smoke," said another.

When it came to Renee's turn, she pulled at the laces of her shoe. She had never missed an assignment and so, focusing on the straightness of these laces, in order to avoid the eyes of her teacher, she said, "I know someone who coughs and coughs." This "someone who" was actually her grandmother, who suffered from bronchitis, but the comment was awarded a very solemn nod from Mrs. LaFlamme. And so the class moved on, leaving Renee feeling a new sense of pride, for having gotten away with a lie that was not a lie, as well as the familiar guilt, which followed any sort of confession. She considered many things to be confessional: using the bathroom pass more than once, for example, or when she specified what kind of eggs she wanted at a restaurant.

"I like them to be a little runny," she would say, although the explicitness of this statement made her cringe.

Her little fib caused a commotion later on, in the cafeteria, as the other students crowded around with their lunch trays, wanting to know who this coughing person was. It must have seemed to them very dark, indeed, to have a coughing person in one's life, as if Renee had said that there was a ghost in her attic, or a hobo under her porch.

"But who is it?" they demanded, and Renee heard herself say that it was her stepfather, even though she did not have a stepfather, and then, because the lie had taken off, she added: "His lungs are black." This shocked the children, but they also believed her, because their health teacher had just warned them of the dangers of smoking, had shown them slides of diseased body parts. One photo had showed a set of teeth, bared and yellow with nicotine. It was a disturbing image, not for the unhealthy color of the teeth and gums, which does not frighten children the way that it frightens adults, but for the uncanny absence of lips. The children gaped at her over their trays and made her promise to tell more stories the next day. This surprised Renee, first of all, because she rarely sought the attention of other children, and secondly, because she had not considered herself to be telling stories. It had seemed to her that she was merely making conversation, drawing from some deep reserve of untruths just to get through the moment until someone else decided to speak. The story had ended with her stepfather's tongue falling out onto the hospital floor. It was also black. The doctors placed it in an incubator, next to the very small babies.

The next morning, Renee found a Bible in her locker.

She did not have to guess who had left it there. Arla Hoffman had even fewer friends than Renee. And while Renee's lack of friends was due to her tireless search for adult praise, Arla did not seem to want to impress anyone. She kept a raw head of garlic in her desk, which she snacked on during lessons. She did not recite the Pledge of Allegiance. Instead, she would walk right out of the classroom, proud, like a gymnast. The students disliked her for this, not because they were old enough to have their patriotism challenged, but because it reminded them, every time, of how they were no longer allowed to have holiday-themed parties at school. No more secret Santas, no more Easter candy. Valentines were forbidden, but "special someone" cards were permitted. Arla had opened her desk to a heap of them that year, all very clever in their interpretation of the word *special*, although one simply said, "yer a dag."

After finding the Bible, Renee met Arla standing by her desk.

"I believe this is yours," she said. Arla was a skinny girl with narrow, reddish eyes. She took the Bible and placed it inside her desk without a word. She was the only person that Renee knew who owned ferrets. Arla had brought three of them in for show-and-tell, transporting them in what looked like a large laundry sack. Ever since, Renee thought she saw a resemblance between the girl and her pets: a kind of twitchy boredom.

Arla had horses too, which was why, shortly after the Bible incident, Arla had invited Renee to go riding; she could come over the next day, if it was all right with Renee's parents.

"It will be a fun activity," she had added, as though reading from a cue card. Her eyes had narrowed as she waited for an answer. A thick-skinned look, like a drowsy lizard in the sun. Over dinner, Renee found herself defending Arla to her parents.

"We didn't know you were friends with her," Renee's father had said through a mouthful of food. It was a rule in Renee's house that no one was allowed to chew with their mouth open, except for Renee's father, who had sinus problems.

"We don't have to be friends to go riding," Renee had said. The argument felt very sound to her. She had an urge to repeat herself, just to hear the evenness of her own voice. She took a bite of food and chewed it slowly, looking at her father.

"Horses can be very dangerous," said Renee's mother.

"A horse has to close its mouth entirely before it opens it again. Imagine what that would do to your finger."

"Arla's horses wouldn't do that," said Renee. She knew that this argument was not as sound but discovered that it did not matter. Just by saying it, she had inadvertently committed herself to liking the girl.

Arla's was the last bus stop, far into the woods, where the bus had to turn around on a steep stretch of road in a maneuver that made Renee sick to her stomach. Once off the bus, the girls walked up a deeply rutted road. It was late March, and the green or newly yellow shoots were pushing up the leaves. The woods smelled dank, Renee thought, like a wet dog. They soon came to a house on a bare patch of ground. The horses were immediately visible, off to the side, their mud-streaked backsides protruding from a lean-to. Burrs were clumped along their tails, and Renee could see gray balls of mud clinging to the hair around their hooves.

Chickens roamed around the front step. They perked up when they saw the girls and surrounded them, trembling with hope that something would be dropped. If they had any emotion to show, it was revealed through their feet, which lifted and lowered with great dexterity and feeling.

"The guinea hens were worse," Arla said as she shut the front door against the cooing chickens. In her delight at having a visitor, it seemed, Arla had become aloof. She kicked off her shoes and walked across the kitchen to the refrigerator. There was something not quite finished about the interior of the house. Areas in the kitchen were exposed: some of the cupboards did not have doors, cans of food were stacked in the corners, and there was a large patch of plaster on the wall by the window. A rotary telephone clung to the wall with a clean, yellow shell. And there were no curtains. Not anywhere. Arla came back with two paper cups of lemonade and the girls drank, right there, on the welcome mat.

After a moment, Mrs. Hoffman entered the kitchen, carrying a small child. She smiled at Renee in a friendly, expectant way, as if someone had just told her that Renee was good at telling jokes. Mrs. Hoffman put the child down and the little girl walked over to Renee, took her hand, and then lifted it to her mouth so that she could suck her thumb and hold Renee's hand at the same time. The three of them—Arla, Renee, and the little girl—made their way upstairs, to Arla's room. On the wall, along the stairway, there was a series of school portraits, three of Arla wearing a large bow in her hair, and a number of pictures of an older boy with straight-cut bangs. The boy got older as they climbed the stairs, and Renee had a considerable amount of time to look at him, as she was still holding the hand of the small child. She watched as his chin became more pronounced, then, all of a sudden, pimply, his teeth larger. She felt vaguely embarrassed for him, that his features were on display like that. It was like watching a potato grow above ground.

The ferrets lived in Arla's room, in a tall cage with many levels. Renee saw the familiar masked faces peering out of a fleece tube inside the cage. Their noses were pale pink, almost white. There was a strong odor upon entering the room, which Renee attributed to the ferrets, and in the corner by the closet, she spotted a pile of something like a clump of tar, which she could not identify. The little girl unclasped her hand and went to the full-length mirror by the bed, stepping over piles of laundry. She stood in front of the mirror and Renee watched the reflection of her face become weepy, drawn in an almost clown-like frown. The girl turned her head from side to side and her frown became even more pronounced.

"Tabbie likes to practice her sad faces," Arla said, still aloof. She opened the cage and three ferrets slid out and began to scamper around the room. They had a way of moving, of veering this way and that, as if their front and hind legs were not completely in accordance. One of them wandered over to the closet and defecated in the corner and Renee understood what the tarry substance had been. I know someone who, she found herself thinking, although she didn't fully understand why.

"One of these guys got his head smashed in the door," Arla said and snatched up a ferret, studying its face. She dropped it and it ran off with its back arched, as if it had broken a bone and didn't care. Arla picked up another and held it at eye level.

"This one," she said, and she gave it to Renee. The ferret's claws were sharp on her bare arms, like a kitten's. Renee looked into its face and saw only that squinty look of tolerance, the same look that Arla had when she marched out of class in the mornings. Renee imagined Arla sitting in that quiet hallway, hearing the school-wide squeal of chairs being pushed back, the soft crackle of the loudspeaker followed by a sea of voices, reciting the lines that, although they had never crossed her lips, she must have known by heart. Renee envied this exemption. It was hard for her to imagine that it might not be Arla's own design that set her apart from the other students. To Renee, it was all Arla, this focused courage that allowed her to sit while others stood, to stare ahead while others laughed. She did not even celebrate her own birthday. It was a feat of tremendous self-control.

The horses were waiting at the gate when the girls stepped out into the backyard. Tabbie had gone back to her mother, who had scooped her up and buried her rosy face into the child's stomach. Renee was not accustomed to displays of affection and ascribed it to something rural, as if affection were like raising pigs: earthy and commendable. She could still smell the rye scent of her father's beard when he would bend down to kiss her goodnight, the uncomfortable sensation of being cherished. After he left, she'd throw off the heavy covers and wait for the kiss to evaporate, rising into the dark room.

"Watch out," Arla was saying. She had gotten hold of a very long whip, which she held with one hand, while hugging an armload of hay. Renee watched as she pushed open the gate with her shoulder and began to wave the whip around above her head. The horses, she saw, were hardly afraid, although they kept just enough distance so that they would not get whacked. They nipped the air with large bared teeth, ears flat to their heads. Arla, it seemed, was looking for a good patch of ground, where the mud was hard enough and where there were fewer piles of manure. She found a spot by a large water trough and tossed the hay down, away from herself, so that the rabid horses would not run her over.

While the horses ate, the girls got to brush them. It was a great task to rake up the dried mud and dust from their hides. Renee was surprised at the force with which Arla went to work, grinding the teeth of her metal brush into the horse's rump, around the base of its tail, which lay flat, tolerantly, now that there was hay to be eaten. They massaged, scraped, and smacked the dirt from those horses, until Renee felt the hot prick of sweat around the collar of her sweater. She set down her brush and pulled the sweater over her head. It clung to her shirt and she accidentally pulled both layers up past her armpits. Arla stared.

"Does your mother know that you are growing

breasts?" she asked. Her arms were at her sides. There was something a bit robotic about Arla, the way emotions seemed to shed from her as soon as they were born. Renee covered her chest with her sweater.

"Am not," she said.

Arla did not argue. "I can show you how to stop them," she said. But Renee just shook her head. They continued brushing. They brushed until the sun began to set and Renee's mother showed up, her station wagon coming to a lopsided halt with one tire resting in a pothole.

"How was your ride?" she wanted to know when Renee was in the car. Renee shrugged. She felt somehow defensive, as though their failure to finish brushing the horses validated her mother's doubt from the night before.

At home, her mother sat down at her sewing machine to make a quilt from some of Renee's old dance-recital costumes, which were flimsy and sequined and did not take to being cut, the material bunching around the scissors. Last week, she had created a throw pillow from a baby blanket. These creations were hideous, but it did not seem to matter. What was important was the tying together of the end of an era. There would be no more dance recitals, no more babies. Everything had its proper retirement. It would have bothered her mother to know that the girls had spent all their time simply brushing the horses, just as she was often irritated at Renee for surfing channels on the TV, never getting to the point. So Renee told her mother how they had ridden through the fields behind Arla's house, how they had leaped over a little stream by the tree line, until one of the horses had started limping and they were forced to go back. It all sounded so convincing that she had to stop herself from fabricating more. The horses, she said, were named Dusty and Moe.

Yes, she thought, just likely enough.

The next week, Renee found herself on the bus to Arla's house again. They sat in the back and watched as the other children were dropped off, one by one, by rows of mailboxes and long driveways lined with dirty mounds of snow. When they came to the end of the road, the bus had to turn around, backing up that steep drive again, like a ship peaking on a wave. Renee's stomach lurched.

She wondered if they were going to ride that day, if they would have time to. Arla sat beside her with her eyes forward, the light fuzz of her profile glowing with sun. They rarely spoke in school. In gym class, when they played dodgeball, Arla threw the ball with inert, brutal force. In music, she blew on her recorder until her cheeks were red. You couldn't say that she was doing a bad job. She hit all the marks. You couldn't say that she wasn't trying. Still, there was something that bothered Renee about her new friend, as if her attitude was a mark of an acknowledged superiority, a snobbishness that Renee felt had not been earned.

The ferrets were already out of their cage, tunneling through laundry on the floor, when the girls got to Arla's room. Renee noted the same foul odor as the week before and hoped that they would go outside soon.

"I want you to tell me something," Arla said, taking a seat on her bed. She had a ferret in her lap. It ducked its head, blinking, every time her hand came down to stroke it. "I want you to tell me about the end of *Fantasia*." Renee did not know what Arla was talking about. She assumed that "the end of Fantasia" had something to do with religion, like the End Times, or the Rapture— subjects that left Renee feeling claustrophobic, because she imagined that the kind of people who believed such things felt a perverse pleasure in believing them. These imaginary people were old and impenetrable and conceited. They brought up God as a parent might mention an embarrassing memory, in an aggressive and precious way. It made Renee's face hot to think of it. She said, "I don't know anything about that."

"Yes you do." The ferret twisted in Arla's hands and flopped onto the floor. "I know you've watched it." It occurred then to Renee that her friend was referring to the film *Fantasia*, with Mickey Mouse. Renee had indeed seen *Fantasia* and would for the rest of her life associate Igor Stravinsky's "The Rite of Spring" with the agonized, sweltering faces of dinosaurs facing extinction. Also, her mother had no opinions about the movie.

"I don't know what you like so much about it," her mother would say, halfheartedly, and then stare at the television for a good five minutes, tapping her finger to the music, as if her mind had been erased. Renee's mother was surprisingly fastidious about music, especially when it came to Christmas music. On December 1, the Christmas tapes would come out and so would begin the most solemn time of year in Renee's household. Her mother's favorite was "The Coventry

Carol," which went "Bye-bye lully lullay," in mourning for infants doomed to die. She liked anything minor in key with the word *sinner* in it. Renee did not necessarily dislike these songs. She found that they gave Christmas a kind of dark history, a bleak, esoteric quality, complicated even further by her mother's atheism.

"You may believe in God if you want to," Renee's mother had said, as if God were an ugly hat.

Renee knew that Arla was talking about the last segment of the film, "Night on Bald Mountain," in which a giant devil with black, flexing wings stirred up demons and summoned spirits from their graves. Of course Arla would not have been allowed to watch that part, Arla, who was sheltered from the mention of Santa Claus and the Easter Bunny. Arla, who was afraid that someone might accidentally give her a birthday present. Renee began to describe the scene, while Arla listened, hungry and alert, like her classmates had been when Renee told the story about her stepfather and the black lung. Her eyes widened and her mouth became slack, completely unguarded, as if her tongue might slide gradually out. She reminded Renee of the large fish in Woolworths, which was too big for its tank and merely flopped itself back and forth, staring in wonder out one side and then the next, as though it could not keep up with the changes in the world. Renee stopped talking. She felt embarrassed—for Arla's sake—similar to the self-consciousness that she felt whenever sex was discussed: that tingling fear that your features will reveal anything more than stony comprehension. She could not go on, not if Arla was going to break open in front of her like an egg.

"Let's ride the horses," she suggested and was relieved when Arla seemed to shake off her trance. And so the girls went outside to the paddock, where the horses were standing in the mud. They got to work, pushing the teeth of their brushes into the shaggy winter fur. There was much to be done: the horses' tails were bound up in burrs, in fat clumps, like birds' nests, and the bottoms of their hooves were padded with a thick layer of manure. There was mud in their ears, in the creases of their buttocks, and speckled across their bellies. And in the animals' eyes, a distant satisfaction, as if they knew that the girls would never finish in time.

Single

◆

Sometimes I would imagine what it would be like to be single, to have my own room again. A room like in a poem, with soft ponderous light. Curtains. Old-fashioned colors, like faded yellows and olive green. There would be a book open on a tidy desk beside a bed with a single pillow. The only thing that would be fit to occupy this room would be my mind, and my mind would be exquisitely made up, like the bed. I would dress differently, a new, convent-inspired wardrobe of blouses and long skirts. I would take on an attractive plainness with my pale lips and my dark eyes, which would always be strained from reading. Perhaps I would become nearsighted and need glasses. The thought excited me.

◆

We were married in his backyard, on a little postage stamp of grass. The guests sat in tall, upright chairs dragged out from the dining room. Others sat in lawn chairs and one took the swivel chair from his father's office and rolled it across the grass. It had only been ten years ago that Eli and I had stood outside in that very spot, putting on a play for his parents, dressed in his parents' clothes. All that I could remember about the play was that we were supposed to be very old. This was conveyed on his part by a bowler hat and on mine by a kerchief tied below my chin. I had also worn his mother's blue sundress, which was long and straight beneath large shoulder pads and had made me look like a stack of books. Afterward, I had snipped out the shoulder pads with shears, not knowing that in ten years I would be performing the same surgery on my mother-in-law's wedding dress. There was something so potent about that dress, with its pearl neckline and its stiff basque waist. It reminded me of a museum that I had been to once, which held drawerfuls of the many small, fatal objects that have caused choking: buttons, bottle caps, fish bones, and pins, so many pins, I recalled. The dress was similar in its gravity; I was still young enough to believe that the dress was a product of certainty, that it carried the same weight as a medal or a weapon. I still believed that the older generations lived more solidly, with more integrity. They found lovers with intrinsic wisdom. They had all the babies that they were fated to have. It seemed that I was the only person in the world whose life was ruled by chance. Every decision that I made seemed accidental—not that it was wrong, but extremely shaky, as if I had only just teetered into place.

When the play was over, Eli's mother and father had stood on the back stoop, clapping their hands. They praised without understanding, their pride unconditional. I sensed the same response to the wedding. Of course it was lovely, because we were the children and the children were always good. Soon everyone was moving inside to eat tuna casseroles and deviled eggs. Eli's aunts doted on me, while my mother picked an eyelash off my cheek. Eli's father bent down to kiss me and I felt that same uncertainty that I had all my childhood: that no one was genuinely impressed with me, that I had succeeded, once again, at meeting expectations, adorably.

After the wedding, we did not have the money for a real honeymoon, so we spent the night at his grandfather's camp. The place smelled like mildew and we had to haul in our own water, but it was better than watching our guests leave, picking up the house, and then retreating to our tiny apartment above his parents' garage, where we had lived since graduating high school. To stay where we were would have been unbearable. Eli's parents would have watched the small square windows snap on and then off and they would know precisely what was going on up there.

When we arrived, we unlocked the deadbolt and brought in our suitcases. I swept the small porch of its leaves and broke down some of the spider webs, but not all. We sprayed each other with insect repellent so we could sit outside and watch the forest light change under the leaves, remaining there for a long time drinking wine that my father had insisted we bring, although neither of us liked the taste of wine. Then we turned to each other with purple teeth and went inside.

It was hot inside the cabin, but we found that when we opened the windows, the screens were either missing or full of holes. Eli said that he was sensitive to mosquito bites in a way that made it sound as if we had only just met, as if we had just arrived on a first date and he was telling me about his allergies. He scratched his arm to reveal how welts were already forming from our time on the porch. I found a metal fan in the corner and plugged it into the naked outlet. It started up with a harsh rattling, but we soon became used to the sound and accepted the muggy air blown in our direction as relief. Coming here, sitting on the edge of the sagging pull-out couch, scratching our arms and legs, began to feel foolish and reckless which, I suspect, put us in danger of seeing our marriage in the same light.

We opened the second bottle of wine. I cannot say exactly how it came about. It might have been the heat, the white noise from the fan. We couldn't think with all the heat and noise and so we began to talk instead. We said things that could not be taken back. All of this chatter, in this womb-like environment seemed safe at first—daring and intimate.

He did not like to receive presents, he told me. They revealed selfishness on the giver's end, a need for recognition. Also, they were a waste of money. Yes, I agreed. We were thrilled to find that we agreed. We would never give each other a gift, we said, and we felt bold and rebellious.

It was my turn. Holidays, I said. Yes, we both exclaimed. Fuck holidays.

I continued. There had been a man who came into the bakery where I worked. He was older. I could only tell because his whole face changed when he smiled. All the excess showed up around his eyes, which were dark and lively, drawing attention with somewhat annoying success. What I was trying to say was that I thought he was handsome. I thought men in general were handsome. In fact, I was in love with men, with their private pain, their beautiful insecure faces, their tricks of confidence. This was okay with Eli. He understood and would not be threatened. He understood, because there was something he'd always wanted to try. He paused and crossed his legs. He reminded me of someone at a party speaking about politics, someone who wanted to convey boredom about his own radical positions.

"I've always liked the idea of being watched," he said. Yes, of course. This was where the conversation was always meant to lead. Sex. We had not talked about sex. We rarely ever spoke of sex. Once, I had told him to keep his finger out of my belly button. We had been young, maybe sixteen. Having known each other throughout our childhood, this move into a romantic relationship was a time for crossing boundaries of all kinds. Now we could kiss, touch. I had allowed

him to be in the bathroom while I peed, which we had
once done unintentionally as children, but neither of
us wanted to admit to remembering. The finger in the
belly button seemed to be a kind of experiment, a test to
see first whether I would tolerate it and, second, to find
out if ours was a safe kind of intimacy, where chances
could be taken. My objection came as a surprise to him.
Surely, he must have thought, I could not have found it
more invasive than some of the other acts that we had
already performed, which meant that it had something
to do with me, a part of myself that he had yet to make
sense of. I couldn't remember how I had put it, whether
it was "Please don't do that" or something sharper, but
I do know that the word *allowed* had not been part of
it. Eli had introduced it when he asked if there was any
other part of my body that he was not allowed to touch.
No, I had said. Neither one of us was to blame for his
reaction, the insult to his pride, but still, I could not
forget it altogether. It was in the language that we used
with each other—*allowed* now meant something more,
it carried with it a hint of resentment. It was a spot that
would never be filled, like a bubble on the inside of a
glass of water.

"I mean watched by a woman," Eli continued. He

said this softly, almost nobly, as if it were for my own protection. I understood. It couldn't be a man.

"But who?" This was the most important question. I imagined a nicely dressed woman—a librarian type—sitting upright in a chair with her hands folded across her skirt. Surely this was not what he meant.

"I guess I hadn't thought that far," he said, although we both knew that this was a lie. Somehow we could not return to where we had just been, to that atmosphere of confidence that we had just had, with the fan roaring, our hot, unconcerned bodies splayed across from each other.

"I've never liked your mother," Eli said.

"I've never really liked either of your parents," was my response. I felt defensive, suddenly, upset that he had chosen this direction. It was not a productive thing to say—that he did not like my mother—he might as well have stated that he did not like the color of my hair, or the size of my breasts. My response had not been out of spite, but had been obligingly honest. I had to deliver it. And in doing so, I found that I did not want to be friendly. That night, I wanted to watch something fall apart, the same way you might have the urge to throw a rock at an ice-covered pond.

I said, "They're the kind of people that think they turned out okay."

"Think they turned out okay?"

"Yeah. And they're smug about it."

When I woke the next morning, the sunlight had turned the curtains an electric green, and in this light, the cabin looked even more dire than the evening before. The floor was heaped with boxes of Sterno cans, bulk toilet paper, and folded gray rugs. The rugs reminded me of something that you might want to pile on if you were freezing in a trench, something fit for a large wet horse. There were things that I could not see from where I lay but that I was well aware of, like the dried bodies of insects, flaking into dust on the windowsills, the splintered, fist-sized hole in the wall next to the woodstove.

Eli slept with his mouth open. It was like a child's, soft and expectant without any stubble surrounding it. He was two months older than I, but only because he had been born prematurely. We had heard this story many times by his mother, how he had been so small that his father could hold him in his palms. Everyone had been worried sick. So he was not really older, we had said when we were children, no. He had been shorter as well, until he turned seventeen, when, suddenly, he grew quite tall and thin. We were both pleased by this, although I was sometimes envious of his slenderness. It seemed that even his wrists, which were hairless, had grown longer and more delicate. I sometimes felt overly plump. He could not lift me and when I sat on his lap, I worried that I was hurting his bones. If only I were thinner, I often thought, then we would be a better match. I could not fathom that maybe it was more fitting this way, that it would be almost comical if we were both slouched and scrawny with our messy black hair. We would look like a rock band, a comic strip.

Eli awoke while I was using the outhouse.

"I thought we were back home," he said when I came back. "You weren't here, so I thought it must be the day of the wedding—you know, because the groom isn't allowed to see the bride." He draped his arm over me and I could smell the sour, evaporated smell of last night's alcohol on his breath and, somehow, in his armpits as well. His kiss was heavy, as if he could not properly predict my distance—and perhaps he could not. It was possible that he was still drunk. It was possible that he remembered nothing from the night before.

We folded up the bed, so that we could sit and have our breakfast. There was no coffee. We talked about what we would do, whether we would walk back down the road, for there was no more road to walk up, and decided that this would feel too much like going home, which, in the end, was what we really wanted. It wasn't that we were unhappy, we assured each other, but that it was never meant to be a real honeymoon in the first place. We had just needed a destination and the camp had fulfilled that. What we needed now was an excuse, because we were not looking forward to the inevitable flash of concern on his parents' faces when we pulled into the driveway. We felt defensive just thinking about it. What if our early return was mistaken for unhappiness, or something worse, like youthful ignorance? We would be like children again, playacting. *And here we go on our honeymoon*, we'd say, skipping over the property line. *And now we are back*, skipping back over, holding hands.

We decided that Eli would be the one to feign illness, because he, being the man, would be taken more seriously. His illness would not be misconstrued as doubt, or regret, or fear. So we dressed and closed up the suitcases, which had not been unpacked in the first place, and took them to the car.

◆

We made it home before lunch and much to our relief, there was no one around to question us. The neighbor had chickens and other strange, rubber-faced fowl that roamed freely between yards and out into the road. As Eli and I got out of the car, the birds moved toward us up the driveway, their heads low and their long feet opening and closing in soft, suspicious steps. It seemed as though they were not completely convinced that we were real. There was another group of chickens over by the spot where the ceremony had been performed. They scratched at the grass in a kind of jerking moonwalk and pecked, hurriedly, as if trying to erase something that had been on the ground.

The front door of the apartment had a little stoop and a porch light fitted with a dark yellow globe. It was my favorite part of the house. Sometimes, sitting out there on a summer evening, I felt as though life were very cozy and livable. It was there that I often became excited about the future, about all the small domestic triumphs that lay ahead. The door led to a stairway that took us above the garage and into a kitchenette with a wood floor. I also liked the small square window above the sink, how it seemed older than the rest of the building with its wavy panes of glass. I imagined that I might look out onto a quaint village square through a window like that, or a small walled garden. In reality, it was my mother-in-law's stretched-out tomato plants and three dusty cabbages that I saw whenever I did the dishes. This wasn't bad or even disappointing, it just didn't fill me with nostalgia, or repose, or any of the feelings that I wanted to sink into when I came home.

The rest of the apartment was set up like a college dorm, with a flat-screen television propped up on two black crates. The walls were covered with posters that Eli picked up from his job at the video rental. *The Usual Suspects*, *12 Monkeys*, *Reservoir Dogs*, *Fear and Loathing in Las Vegas*. These films could be found on another small bookshelf beneath the window along with other VHS tapes and DVDs, all of which held great significance and genius. There were lines to be memorized, camera tricks to be worshipped, rewound, and explained to me. And I did not dislike this. It was just that there was something inherently masculine and alienating about the whole thing, as if part of Eli's love for the movies was the fact that I could never completely understand them—and what kept me from fully appreciating them was his confidence that I could not. A wire bookshelf held the majority of Eli's comic book collection. The rest he kept in plastic sleeves in an ugly cardboard box next to the bed, labeled *Eli's Comics*, as if it weren't obvious, as if they were not always right *there*, the first thing he saw every morning. The first thing that I would see every morning from now on.

When I left Eli a month later, his reaction was unexpectedly cold. He seemed to believe that cleaning the apartment would protect him from the pain of it, as if I had somehow always been a hindrance to his idea of perfection.

"Look how clean the place is," he said to me when I went back to pick up the rest of my belongings. He was standing in the living room. Light was seeping in through the closed blinds, as if through a layer of water, and I had the eerie feeling that we had just encountered each other at the bottom of a lake.

"Look how clean the place is," he said again, and there was something ghostly about him, standing there in the half-light with his hands clasped. Eli liked to be overly careful and mild whenever we had a fight. He had a gentle, terrible anger, and here it was again. He had cleaned and there was a morbid pride in it. *See what I am without you—so pure and unsullied.* The light, at that angle, seemed to slip into the irises of his eyes as if from the side, like light through a marble. They were so blue and limpid and I remember thinking, Another irretrievable thing.

I made sounds, I hollered and wept and pried open something dark and robust, like a fallen tree pulling up the ground. There was a smell to my sorrow that seeped from my skin, my sweaty palms, and my swollen eyes, like soil that has been plowed. That was me, in my mess, and here was Eli, with his white carpets and his bleached windowsills.

Before we were married, when we were just living together as boyfriend and girlfriend, I had caught him taking pictures of me through the frosted glass of the shower door, my body a pale blur, like a fish under ice.

"What are you doing?" I had wanted to know. I came out dripping, water streaming down my arms to the tips of my fingers, droplets blinking on my eyelashes.

"Take the picture now," I had said, standing there bristling with goose bumps, and he'd brought the camera to his eye, but he could not do it. The day I went to collect my things, he showed me how white he'd gotten the bottom of the shower, the brightness of the grout between the tiles.

"Look," he said, and he showed me my corner of the bedroom that had always been piled with clothes, strewn with the black bandit masks of my underwear. That patch of rug was bare, the tassels straight, as if someone had come round with a comb. I was not hurt or alarmed, but rather relieved, as if I'd come across bones that had been picked clean. Here was the very end of it, the absence of decay or unsightly emotional things. I took up my box of possessions—two cookbooks that I had never used, a small houseplant, and a wad of folded letters that I had written to him that he no longer wished to keep. I imagined that the sight of my wiry penmanship straying in and out of the lines would offend his senses. Best to get rid of it, as if it were something thorny and invasive. It was then that I thought to ask for the photos. He shrank back.

"You can't tell that it's you," he said sheepishly, and I saw that light creeping sideways into the blue of his eye.

"Maybe," I said, "but they were taken without my permission."

"Some of them," he said.

It was true.

After I'd caught him, he had told me to get back into the shower. I had thought that he would follow me, but he stayed just on the other side of the door with his camera, telling me what he wanted to see—a hip or a breast, the palm of my hand—and I would place that part against the glass and it would appear to him flattened and white. From inside the shower, I could not hear the click of his camera, but I could see him bring the dark box up to the blur of his face as I repositioned myself against the cold glass. When, at last, the pile of photos was in my hand, I dropped them into the box and I left the apartment and Eli standing there, knowing that he would probably vacuum the spot on the carpet where I had walked with my shoes.

It was raining when I got into my car. I tossed the box onto the passenger seat beside me and drove until my curiosity became too great. I pulled off to the side of the road where there was a wide shoulder, a place that I knew people to park in the summer and walk down through the trees to the river. I turned the keys in the ignition and the wipers froze halfway across my windshield and the hard drops of rain turned the glass thick and murky and jumping with water. I felt for the pile of photographs and placed them on my lap and there I was, shrouded in steam, each picture drawing attention to a new part of me, that slab of flesh pressed up against the glass of the shower door unnaturally, as if I was looking at meat trapped under cellophane. There was my breast, a fish eye, flat and wary. My belly, a strange oyster. I could not imagine what had compelled Eli to keep these images. They were not beautiful, or womanly, or artistic in any way. I could rip them up and take them down to the river where they would be washed away in little white flakes. I could simply leave them on a boulder and let the rain bead over their glossy surfaces. Eli was right, there was nothing in the photos to identify me. It wouldn't have mattered if someone found them. I could have allowed him to keep them, allowed his memory of me to become cool and bleary until there was nothing left but these amphibious blobs of flesh.

Rodeo

◆

The other mothers covered their children's eyes. April covered her son's ears. She might have expected the horse to cry or to struggle, gasp for breath. She had never seen a horse lie down before; this one had fallen flat on its side.

Douglas shook his head free from his mother's hands. "Are they going to stop the show?" he asked.

The horse didn't move.

April noticed that the other mothers had started to pack up and guide their children down the bleachers. The horse needed his rest, a big Band-Aid. There were offers of cartoons before bedtime. April wondered why she had not considered leaving.

"Keep that horse down, boys!" the announcer shouted

over the loudspeaker as three men in cowboy hats ran in from the gates. The men dashed to the lifeless animal and sat on the body, as if to keep it from flailing. A man on the horse's rump waved to the crowd in what was most likely an attempt to say, *Everything's all right, folks!*

"We can go home if you'd like," April said, keeping her eyes on the arena. There was a cowboy at the horse's head, stroking its cheek. The man's lips were moving.

"I think its neck broked," said Douglas.

April could only nod. The horse had thrown its rider with a vertical twisting motion, flashing the undersides of its hooves, then took off at a gallop across the open arena, still slick from the morning's rain. Right before it reached the fence, it had lost its footing and landed on its head, balancing for a moment, it seemed, on the white star between its eyes. All this happened quickly and clumsily, which was to be expected of an animal of that size, but also, April thought, far too easily, like a child falling down.

A tractor pulling a horse trailer roared through the gate.

"Now we can get this ol' boy the help he needs," said the announcer, slow and soothing. "Yes, folks, we're gonna be all right here."

"How do you help a broked neck?" Douglas asked quietly. April saw that he was looking down at his hands. She wondered if the damage was already done, if Douglas would grow up with some kind of weird phobia. She had not brought her son to the only rodeo in Vermont to pick up more worries.

There was something wrong with April's husband, or at the very least, something about him was different. Paul was mild-mannered and somewhat old-fashioned in his habits. When he returned home from work, he changed from his shirt and tie into his "house" clothes—a new button-up and a pair of slacks that did not look to April to be any more comfortable—and then, at bedtime, into his pajamas, which sometimes he ironed. He was never outspoken, but April knew that he carried within him a long list of opinions that he would not like to be challenged, by her, or by anyone. He was like a well-made box: sturdy, uncomplicated, and with a clearly defined purpose—on the outside, at least.

April would sometimes have a reoccurring dream. In the dream, the hospital called to tell her that Paul had been crippled in a motorcycle accident—a motorcycle that she had not known about. She was obliged to give him sponge baths and little bites of baby food. The dream always ended with her looking for vegetables to mash for his dinner.

They both laughed whenever she had the dream, as if the motorcycle—his big secret—was a mark of their own lack of imagination, their old couple's humdrum.

"A motorcycle?" Paul kidded her. "That was the best you could come up with?"

Paul had never touched a motorcycle. Paul rode a bicycle. He rode it to his office, a slate-roofed building with a row of decapitated hedges along the walkway. Once there, he would go into the bathroom to pat his hair down with water and reapply his deodorant stick, just in case the short, downhill commute had caused him to break a sweat.

"Check his desk for a flask," April's friend Roxanne had said in the early days of their relationship. "All lawyers are depressed. They have to be."

Roxanne had been a prosecutor, turned public defender, and then gave up law altogether to be a middle-school woodshop teacher.

"A classroom of tweens with table saws?" she loved to say. "Try dealing with a judge for a day."

At the beginning of every school year, Roxanne would hold up her right hand and wait for the hush to fall over the classroom, as her students, one by one, noticed the red jagged line, the mangled stump of pinkie, like a fleshy chess pawn.

"Be alert," she'd tell them, "and you won't have to find out how this happened." She had been ten years old when her uncle's pet iguana, Lizzy, bit off her finger, but her woodshop class didn't have to know that.

April had found no flask in Paul's office, just a number of cryptic—although mundane—handwritten sticky notes. "File the straw." "Half-wit prairie dog." "Rock-a-bye Paper Plane." A bit jarred, but not wanting to seem meddling, she had tried her best to forget them.

"Broken," said April.

Douglas peered at her. "What?"

"Broken, not broked. The neck is broken," she said, as if from a grammar text.

"Well, how do you fix it?"

It took six men to haul the horse into the back of the trailer. It happened quickly, as if they had all done it before. April watched the tractor speed out the gate, its tires flinging mud onto the first row of onlookers. She was wondering how to answer Douglas's question. When he was born, April had resolved to always tell her son the truth, no matter how difficult the subject. Once the boy was old enough to ask questions, however, she had been shocked by her urge to lie and to lie extravagantly. It had come as strongly as her need to slice his grapes in half so he would not choke on them, to kiss his knees when he fell.

"You don't," she said.

April taught middle-school English, a thankless task, far from her dreams of well-loved copies of *The Catcher in the Rye* and perfectly sharpened pencils. Instead, her desk drawers buzzed with confiscated cell phones and her hands were always parched with chalk. Year after year, her students stared from their seats, like frogs blinking in the water. The only students that liked her were boring, desperate for an A because it was all that they could comprehend.

Sometimes April thought that Roxanne was cheating, with that finger of hers. Roxanne's students offered up birdhouses, jewelry boxes, and little wooden letter

*R*s, rapt at her every word, as if it might earn them a bit of her magic.

"And now the moment you've all been waiting for." The announcer roared on through his script. Barrels were rolled through the dirt; the gusto of the crowd was up. Anyone too upset to keep watching had gone.

The gates were opened and a pony scrambled through, as if it had been running like that for miles. The young rider had her hands all the way up by its ears, gripping the reins, pumping the air. They took the first barrel at such a tilt that the girl's toe made a line in the dirt. April felt a twist of apprehension. What if another horse goes down? She wondered if it would make things worse, or rather, if the two instances, by the laws of absurdity, would nullify each other.

That morning, Roxanne and April had gone shopping together, an outing that had more to do with giant lattes and little cakes than anything else.

"You deserve this," Roxanne said as she drove them downtown. Her hand on the steering wheel reminded

April of a half-mangled starfish, clinging to a rock. She had heard somewhere that starfish could grow back lost limbs, but she didn't dare confirm the theory with Roxanne, who would expose her train of thought in an instant. Instead, April found herself putting words behind something that she hadn't wanted to express to anyone.

"There's something wrong with Paul," she said, "but don't ask me what. I don't know."

Roxanne's expression remained placid, as if she had been expecting this. She glanced over her shoulder to change lanes and April stole another peek at the stunted pinkie, stretching taut the red, scarred skin.

"Tell me this, then." Roxanne was almost monotone. It meant that she wasn't planning for them to become too engrossed in the subject. "How do you know?"

"He said something." What April wanted to say was that he'd said something that she hadn't expected, but she worried that it would sound unimaginative, or rigid.

The first time April had tried to tell Roxanne about the motorcycle dream, her friend had waved her hands around her ears.

"Don't even bother," she had said. "I can never pay attention. And besides, all dreams are about impotence. Especially dreams about impotence."

They stopped at a strip mall, in a random bracket of the nearly deserted parking lot, where the rain was starting to pool oily and black. It was always in parking lots that April forgot everything that she had intended to buy, where the practice of moving goods from one location to the next suddenly lost its charm. In the end, it was the fear of not wanting anything, the empty-handed finality of it, that kept her from turning around and going home.

When they pulled up in front of April's house, Paul was ready with an umbrella.

"She's all yours," Roxanne said, handing him the last of April's shopping bags.

"And what if I don't know what to do with her?" he asked. He had probably expected an appreciative snort from April's friend, at the very least, but Roxanne had already turned around and was standing on the front porch, tucking waves of dark hair under her hood, about to step into the rain. She pointed her key and followed it to the door of her car, leaving the couple alone with Paul's question, like a pair of teenagers forced into a closet at a party, devastatingly aware of each other.

◆

Douglas needed to use the bathroom, but the line wasn't moving. From where they stood, on a path of crushed straw and hardened mud, April could still see the glowing white numbers of the mounted digital timer. The man on the horse had only lasted two seconds before he was thrown. April wondered if it was the lack of buildup, of gladiatorial narrative, that had made the whole scene so pathetic. Death was fussy and then it was over. It didn't make for a very good show.

"Number one or number two?" A man in muddied chaps and a cowboy hat was sitting on his heels in front of Douglas. April recognized him as the man who had been stroking the fallen horse's cheek.

"I mean," he leaned in for a loud whisper, "do you need to go number one or number two?" Douglas looked at his mother and lifted one sheepish finger. The man stood, this time addressing April.

"I can guarantee that my horse's stall is a hundred times cleaner than that sludge heap." He indicated the dented porta-potty at the head of the line. "I'd be happy to show you," he said. Then, perhaps realizing how his offer must sound, he added, "That is, if y'all are comfortable with that."

April and Douglas followed the man into a long barn

with two facing rows of iron-barred stalls. Yellow light-bulbs, stuck sideways from posts, lit their way, while around them horses nudged their long faces into feed bags, crunching. The barn brought a welcomed hush after the roar of the stadium, and April could feel the hollow of nostalgia start to open within her chest. She'd grown up with two goldfish and a classroom hermit crab, nothing like these gassy, grumbling beasts. And yet there she was, stirred by the promise of something familiar.

The man led a clean, chestnut-colored horse from one of the stalls by a halter, tied loosely over its flaring muzzle. It stood patiently, blowing dust, while Douglas shuffled into the stall. April could see that the man had been right; the horse's space was kept impeccably clean, with heaping mounds of fresh wood shavings, smelling of pine. Still, she knew it put Douglas in an awful spot, forced to choose the humiliation of peeing in the presence of a stranger over the humiliation of wetting himself.

"Quite a night for the little guy," the man said, dropping his head toward the now-closed stall door. April felt a small shock of guilt; they could have easily taken the first exit to a rest stop or grocery store, she knew, but she had been following her own selfish curiosity.

◆

It had happened in the middle of the night: a strange whimpering that shook April from her sleep. She thought at first that Douglas had come into their bedroom, frightened by a dream, but she had opened her eyes to a closed door, an empty bedside. It came again, this time punctuated by short gasps, like the metal wheezing of an old mattress. When Paul sat up beside her, April assumed that he had heard it too, but he didn't speak. The strange wheezing was his laughter.

The bedroom was tinted blue from the moon-shaped nightlight in the baseboard outlet. Now, to April, the color looked cold, falling over Paul's features, making his skin appear thin, the grooves of his ear unfamiliar— absurd—like a word said aloud too many times. April did not want to see him like this, like the Paul that she had known, that she had been married to for all these years, was breaking open.

When he spoke, the inside of his mouth was dark.

"I dreamed I was real," he said, studying his palms. He flipped them over. His eyes widened. "I was real." April got out of bed and walked down the hallway to the kitchen, where she filled a tall glass with water from the tap. She brought the glass back to the bedroom and handed it to Paul. She often did the same for Douglas, when he woke from a bad dream and needed comforting. But Paul just gazed at the glass in his hand, as if he had never seen anything like it, then slowly dipped his finger into the water. April did not know what else to do.

"That horse," April began. She needed to know what the man in the cowboy hat had said to it, while he stroked its cheek under the stadium lights.

The man shook his head. "A real shame," he said. "That horse's owner was planning on retiring him next week."

Douglas pushed open the stall door and stepped back into the warm glow of the aisle, his ears rimmed red with embarrassment. Of course they should leave, thought April. They should have been home an hour ago, wrapped in a quilt, drowning the events of the night with ice cream and excessive television.

"I know," said April, leaning down toward her son. "How about some *Frosty the Snowman* when we get home?"

Something dropped inside her son; the weight of

shame upon shame. He looked at the cowboy, then at the floor. She wished that she could undo it all.

They could still hear the voice of the announcer, overlapped in echo, as they walked through the roped-off field to the car. April decided that the man in the cowboy hat must have been singing to the horse. She decided that whatever he had been singing had probably been sacred in the moment but meaningless overall, like the last song he had heard on the radio, or a school anthem. As she and Douglas were leaving the barn, the man had taken a mint from his pocket and fed it to his horse, holding his hand flat beneath the animal's smacking lips to catch the pieces that fell and offer them up again. Douglas, allowed the front seat, frowned under his seatbelt. It'll be all right, thought April. She would ask Roxanne to come over in the morning. Roxanne enchanted Douglas. She'd bring him out to brunch, pressure him into drinking some of her coffee, then buy him something flimsy at the toy store. April disapproved, which was why it was the only remedy.

As she drove away, she watched the dome of light from the rodeo flicker behind the noise of trees and houses until it disappeared. She forced herself to imagine the horse going down, how its back legs had touched the ground by its ears, how it flipped again and then landed, hard. How the man's lips had moved, soft pink, surrounded in stubble. Tender, like a little lie. She was relieved when Douglas dozed, bouncing his cheek against his shoulder. When they reached home, she would carry him inside, take off his sneakers, let him sleep in his jeans. She would find Paul, reading in bed, watch him tuck the jacket of his book into the pages to save his place, and then put the book on the nightstand to show that she had his full attention.

"How was the rodeo?" he would ask, smiling, and April would have no idea how to answer.

Trespassers

◆

The woman on the swing wore an orange plastic sun visor and a pair of flamingo clip-ons, which pinched her earlobes to a similar, if more painful, shade of pink. Her jumper was corduroy, embroidered with a moose on the front pocket, and it reminded the girls of something their second-grade teacher might have worn. The teacher had loved moose and wore moose sweaters and jewelry and had a moose sticker on the back of her car but seemed to have no knowledge of the species beyond its decorative functions. She had laughed at a boy who asked whether the moose on her tote bag was a cow or a bull. For this, the girls had never forgiven her, nor had they forgiven themselves for laughing along. It had been their first lesson in the scarcity of atonement, how it did not fly about like geese searching for water, how their shame would lie, for weeks, open-face to the sky.

The woman in the swing had a voice like a parrot. The strap of her swing was buckled tightly, somewhere between a thick stomach roll and a lower bulge that they had no language to describe. Her toenails were long, and black from skimming the dirt. "Boss, where'd you get to?" she said. "Boss?"

The girls refused to be shocked in each other's company. They came out of the woods lashed by thorns and splotched red from exertion, and they stopped short in front of the chain-link fence, which separated them from the woman in the swing. Catherine carried a sword, which she handled with boredom, as if to say, *Don't ask.* Emi was attempting, awkwardly, to scratch a mosquito bite on her left shin with the toe of her right sandal, but at last she gave up and stood still, her feet splayed out. The sudden and not-quite-perceived arrival of hips was to blame for this stance, as well as an oafish self-consciousness brought on by the propositions of too many older men who confused the rich color of her skin for sexual maturity. If they couldn't place her, it seemed, then she must be old enough. Her name, which throughout her childhood had been a friendly tapering of letters—*E-M-I*, three blueberries in a pail—had lately proved insufficient, its brevity too accessible. The way some people said it was like they had permission.

Catherine buried the blade of her sword into the crumbling flesh of a tree stump. It was a collector's item, ordered from a catalog that also sold pewter dragons and hooded sweatshirts with built-in headphones. Her brother, Camden, had thrown a tantrum when he was told that he would not be allowed to bring it with him to college, and Catherine had decided to punish him— for being a baby—by using the replica to hack through the woods behind their house.

The girls walked the length of the chain-link fence and eyed the big house, a disorderly Queen Anne with a turret that showed its hollowness by placement of windows on either side. There was something about its structure that lacked all the usual indicators of either vacancy or occupancy; it was impossible to tell if someone was watching. The woman laughed at them when they pushed their faces against the fence.

"Hi, little piggies," she said, which embarrassed the girls. It may have been pride that led Catherine to start climbing. Whatever the reason, once she was over, Emi had to follow. Though Emi was taller, it was more difficult for her, and, catching the heel strap of her sandal near the top, she might have been stuck hanging cartoonishly upside down had the leather not snapped and let her fall. This pleased the woman in the swing and she kicked her legs in an attempt to get herself going. She laughed again and Emi saw the inside of her mouth, where the teeth sprawled. It reminded her of the time her uncle plowed their driveway and accidentally drove over the picket fence, bending and splintering the posts in the snow. To make matters worse, it was clear by the woman's papery scalp that she had been sitting in the sun for too long. Her lipstick had gathered in a clump on her bottom lip.

"Boss!" she sang again, swinging her legs. "C'm'ere, boy!" The girls looked around in alarm, but there was no one in the yard. A hanging plant on the back porch gave the impression of a man standing in the shadows. It would catch them off guard another three times before they left.

Their little expedition had not been just about the sword. The girls were also trying to hold on to something that they had shared when they were younger: an unusual thirst for hard work. When they were eleven, they had surprised Catherine's father by building a crude boat from a wooden box and three inner tubes, then paddling it across Parsons Lake. They used snow shovels for oars. Catherine's father had driven them to the lake in his truck, all the while perfecting his "leave it to the professionals" speech for when the time came to haul them out of the water by their pigtails. But they had made it. Half an hour later, they were falling against the opposite shore, hearts like melons, the whole sky rippling around the edge. A man sitting on the dock with his feet in the water threw his head to laugh at them, and they could see the brown pits where he was missing teeth. And when they drove away, their slightly less-intact creation rattling behind them in the bed, Catherine's father sat so silently behind the wheel that the girls felt they must have done something wrong.

Emi and Catherine's projects continued, but they lost energy over the years. By now, they were fifteen and sad about this, but they could not quite grasp that it was not lack of imagination or desire that held them back, but a new and insidious kind of vanity that went far beyond pinching stomach rolls and comparing profiles. Without knowing, they were both cultivating an inner voice that kept a record of every time they were wrong and that whispered to them of small but ruinous embarrassments.

Still, they tried. They had packed Catherine's borrowed camera as well as the contents of her mother's makeup drawer and taken to the woods. The idea was to take suggestive photographs of each other with maybe an artistically placed vine binding their wrists, or across their mouths. They had practiced their "Help me—don't help me" eyes in the mirror. But there were no such vines and, as it turned out, once you stopped walking all the mosquitoes that had been content just to stalk dove in for the kill. So they trudged forth, following the clean swish of Catherine's stolen sword.

It was the summer that Emi went on birth control without her mother's permission. Catherine had driven Emi to the hospital in her father's truck. She would wait, she told Emi, in the hospital's lobby, where there was a large fish tank. Looking into fish tanks, Catherine said, was like watching the opening credits of a lost memory, something that was impossible to retrieve but was achingly close. Sometimes Catherine said beautiful things, and she kept a long list of sentences under her bed that she would one day put into a story, when the time was right, she said.

Emi had sat at the edge of the examining table that day, tugging at the bottom of her paper gown, while the nurse laid two gleaming speculums across a towel.

"This," said the nurse, cradling the smallest in her hand, "this is what we call our 'virgin' model." She sealed her lips in anticipated satisfaction. "But this is what we will be using for you." The nurse held up the second, considerably larger speculum and clapped the jaws, as if planning an act of violence.

The woman was right. Emi was no longer a virgin. It didn't matter that Neil had stopped halfway through the act, left her lying on his bed while he bent over, pale ass to the ceiling, to rummage through a backpack on the floor. His head and shoulders had reappeared and he showed her the digital camera, pressed the button to prove to her that there was no memory chip. He set it on the nightstand on top of a stack of textbooks. The uncovered lens looked on with its empty brain.

"I just like to pretend that someone is watching," he had said and smiled at the camera.

The doctor entered the examining room, picked up a clipboard, set it down. Emi noticed his broad shoulders, his eyes, heavy with knowing. He told Emi to place her heels at the edge of the table, then skootch—he used the word *skootch*—her bottom toward his light.

"Keep going, keep going," he coaxed, until she felt as though she would fall, and then he said, "I won't let you fall." She must have mistaken this last bit for omnipotence, for when the gleam of the speculum made contact, she opened her whole self to him.

The girls had given up on their photography project. It was too bad. They had hoped to use the photos to shock their chemistry teacher, Mr. Albus, who taught black-and-white photography as a short block, whom Catherine had admitted to finding attractive because he once arrived late to class looking as though he had been crying. Catherine, Emi knew, had lost her virginity last fall, to Ricky Bruggs Jr. in a hunting tree stand, which poor Catherine kept mistakenly calling a tree house.

"Sex smells awful" had been the first thing Catherine related over the phone to Emi, only to find out later that the camouflaged sleeping bag that had covered the floor of the stand had been sprayed accidentally with deer urine. To Emi it didn't seem fitting that Catherine—fish tank gazing Catherine—would fool around with Ricky Bruggs Jr., but, according to Catherine, he understood death with a wisdom beyond his years.

Once Catherine put away the camera and took up the sword again, Emi tried to describe to her how the eye of Neil's camera had made her go cold, how she had felt as though she were hovering an inch above herself—a sickening, convulsive feeling, like water made to jump with the force of sound waves. The word *copulation* had come to mind, a frigid piece of vocabulary owned by scholars, not girls like Emi, who, unlike her friend, kept no beautiful lists beneath her bed.

But Catherine only swung her sword, caught it on an evergreen sapling. "So you guys made a sex tape," she said, and she wiggled the blade free. That was when they had heard the voice.

"Boss," it said. "Come home!"

The woman on the swing was smiling, like a child on a carousel horse, pleased, it seemed, to have an audience. Catherine took one of the tubes of lipstick that they had stolen from her mother—a dark color that the girls had decided shouldn't be worn by a woman who says, "Oh, biscuits!" while tripping down a flight of stairs—and offered it to her.

"Stop—" Emi stooped as she spoke, feeling the openness of the yard, the looming pressure of the old house. She could hear the vacant melody of chimes from the back porch, the cicadas in the forest. She studied the fenced yard with its patches of dried grass, a barrel planter in the corner, where someone had attempted a circle of marigolds. The mulch was worn away beneath the swing, where the woman had gotten off to take the lipstick. She applied it, her eyes closed in concentration.

"Got any smokes in there?" Catherine reached into the woman's moose pocket. She pulled out an ID card and read it aloud: "Maxie Mites. Height: sixty-two inches. Weight: one hundred sixty-five. Eye color: hazel." Then she tucked it back into the pocket.

"Maxie Mites. Maxie might what?"

The woman opened her eyes and carefully screwed the lipstick back into the tube. She laughed.

"Maxie—" she managed, breathlessly, then stopped laughing. "Maxie bites." She looked from Catherine to Emi, then back to Catherine, and clapped her jaw, which unnerved the girls enough to climb back over the fence.

◆

In the weeks that followed, they were increasingly troubled by the possibility that they were now trespassers, the kind of girls who would have to carry out the tragic existence of rebels. When it came to Maxie, they agreed on the term *challenged*, because they had no idea who to consult on these matters. Furthermore, they found that it released them from the word *disabled*, which was too permanent a sentence for girls for whom everything still fluctuated: their waistlines, the pores of their skin, the names that they wrote and then crossed out on the inside of their binders. They stargazed with the smugness of those gifted with imagination. They would rather die than fall in love with a celebrity. And, despite themselves, they worried about Maxie, that her play yard behind the old Victorian was actually a prison, her new shade of lipstick a waxy curse.

Their minds were set at ease, weeks later, when they spotted Maxie buying a candy bar at a gas station in town. She was alone, wearing an orange reflective vest. The girls had been sharing a milk shake at a greasy table in the back by the magazine racks—Catherine taking only one sip for Emi's two because she had decided then and there that she was on a diet. Neither wanted to admit how astonished they were at the sight of Maxie, and so they widened their eyes and gaped, masking surprise with surprise.

Maxie made her way down Main Street, eating her candy bar. Every few minutes, she would stop chewing and give a short whistle.

"C'm'ere, boy!" she called, and she stooped to look behind a garbage can. "Boss!" she yelled. "Boss!" There were others on the street, locals, used to this behavior, doing their best to keep an ignorant pace. The girls followed, keeping their distance, pretending to look with interest into shop windows. Emi sipped the remainder of the milk shake and feared, momentarily, that their friendship was in jeopardy, that once they ran out of windows to peer into—fixing their hair, feeling embarrassed by a mannequin for no good reason—that they would come to the end of the street and have nothing left to talk about.

Later, Emi would decide that the end of their friendship had not happened then, but soon after, the day that she had screamed suddenly in chemistry class. Her scream had been so disruptive that the class was dismissed early, and Catherine was pulled out of English by the high school's vice principal. Catherine, Emi imagined, would have been told to gather her books, led down empty hallways to an unknown source of drama, wondering, Is a family member ill, has Ricky Bruggs Jr. been killed in a hunting accident? He had once written her a poem about tracking a wounded deer through the woods. He had rhymed *doe* with *snow* and *thirty below*, but then also *plow*, which Catherine said made it a sophisticated poem. Catherine would have thought of the poem as she walked, guided by that stern presence of the vice principal, a man who defied aging behind a large black moustache. She would have recited the poem under her breath, imagining herself the fated deer, would have hoped, secretly, that Mr. Albus would see her, recognize her as that wounded creature imagined by Ricky Bruggs Jr. but understood, truly, by grown men.

Mr. Albus was there, at the end of the hallway, behind his desk, his chalkboard scrawled halfway with the squashed spiders of chemical compounds. Emi was there too, sitting alone in the back row. She watched Catherine's eyes travel across the empty desks, watched her disappointment turn flat, almost dangerous, as it became clear to her that no one was dead, that it was just her best friend, who, in nursery school, once burst into tears over the word *Cray-Pas*.

"Emi has had a hard morning," the vice principal said from the doorway, and then he left it up to his moustache to convey the understatement.

What Emi had had was an out-of-body experience, though no one else would call it that, not even the psychiatrist that her parents were quick to hire at the urging of a guidance counselor. The psychiatrist had liked the term *dissociation*, which was one of those words that flew out of the gates too fast, like *socioeconomic*.

The first fourteen minutes of chemistry class had passed routinely. Emi, always the good student, had looked over her homework before delivering it to the wire basket on Mr. Albus's desk. Her teacher had given her his pained smile, as if to say, *Would it hurt to be wrong, once in your life?*

The lesson had followed, with Mr. Albus turning his back to them to write on the chalkboard, the class already too bored to find enjoyment in the chalk dust on his elbows. And then he had turned around again, to make one of his points, the kind that could not be put to rest until he had made eye contact with every one of his students.

That was when it began: a queasiness, a doubling of self, very similar to what Emi had experienced in Neil's bedroom. She had not floated, nor had she looked down upon herself, as near-death survivors have claimed, but instead she found that her perspective had shifted, so that Mr. Albus's face was suddenly disproportionately large and very near, even though he remained at the head of the classroom. She saw his face as an insect might, or a baby peering out a fifth-story window during the Macy's parade—confronted by giants, frightfully convex. The eyeballs bulged, like whole moons, rolling in fleshy cauldrons. A mouth opened and she saw that frothing orifice as nothing more than a mechanism for swallowing up worlds. She had thought of the word *behemoth*, watched as it erased all neurological alliances with the words *person*, *man*, *friend*. She had screamed, of course, and clinging to her desk, so as not to be sucked into the void, had accused her teacher, in front of the whole tenth-grade chemistry class, of trying to eat her.

The psychiatrist prescribed her an antipsychotic, which nauseated her in the mornings, which led her mother to ask her if they needed to talk, to which Emi, taken off guard, had replied: "Yes, mother, I have copulated." This led to sobbing—on Emi's part—at the sad relief of confession, the loneliness of finding herself on the other side of her mother's trust, and, of course, that same embarrassment that she had always suffered at the ownership of words that she believed were not hers to own. She was still haunted by *Cray-Pas*.

There was much speculation as to why it had happened. Catherine, for one, had discussed it with Ricky Bruggs Jr., who revealed that sometimes he, too, left his body, to see through the eyes of the animals he hunted. He had seen the world dim around the edges, he said, then plunge into darkness. But you didn't see Ricky Bruggs Jr. running to a shrink.

Then there was Emi's mother, who pattered around outside her daughter's door, day and night, waiting for Emi to emerge and confess that she had been on drugs the whole time.

Neil, naturally, believed that his erection had been the instigator.

"Childhood trauma," said the psychiatrist. He wanted to know if Emi could recall any past occurrences—anything at all that stood out, loose threads that might mar the tapestry of her childhood. Yes, she had told him. There had been one thing.

◆

Emi's parents, like all parents, she had assumed, had a private bookshelf in their bedroom for miscellany—that dirty comic book that would have been thrown out had it not been a gift from her father's close friend—and then a public bookshelf for guests to admire, its contents mundanely bound in reverence to the entryway. Emi was often drawn to this second bookshelf, as though it were a puzzle; surely, if she looked long enough, she would discover something interesting, something grown-up, or at least anatomical. What she had found was a *Birds of North America* guide, pages filled with brown females and white throats. Names like *nuthatch, nightjar, titmouse*; compounds that found safety in odd partnership. And then she had come to the egrets, the ibises, declared them the princesses of the birds, because they were slender and picked fish out of the water in a dance that she knew to be highly selective. She wanted to see these birds in real life, and she let her parents know. They weren't the type of parents to take this news as an opportunity to visit a conservancy or go for a hike, but as permission to yell, pointing out of car windows—"Look! Ah, you missed it."

But one day she hadn't missed it.

"A great blue heron!" her mother had cried, practically screaming. It flew up from the marsh, vertically at first, wings open, as if it would shoot off into the clouds. A skinny angel with an appointment. It wasn't really blue, but gray and white with some black markings. How could Emi explain to her mother the horror, this buildup of expectation—of blueness, of greatness! It wasn't that she was disappointed at the sight of the bird, but that for an instant the gears of recognition jammed and the thing outside her car window, this long figure of ascension, revealed itself to be not a heron— not even a bird—but the specter of life behind feathers. It stretched out of the murk, like a twiggy soul leaving the body, and Emi had shut her eyes, fists in her sockets, so that she wouldn't have to see anymore.

The psychiatrist did not see how this was relevant.

In the wake of Emi's confession to her mother, she was no longer allowed to visit Neil at his house. They spent the remainder of the warm days walking, to the gas station for milk shakes, through the graveyard, or on that one glass-strewn path to the river, where it wasn't the village of tarps and clotheslines or the still-smoldering cigarette in the mud that frightened them, but the sight of human feces, wrapped loosely in newspaper. Neil suggested that they go to the park, maybe watch the boys crash their BMX bikes on the track. This did not seem appealing to Emi, but Neil insisted.

"It will be very funny," he said, humorlessly, and Emi knew not to question this tone. The instinct rose from her gut, a silvery impulse that flashed, like a mother's warning.

There was one, much younger, boy at the park, who did not ride on the track but pedaled aimlessly between the swings, once placing the front wheel at the base of the slide, timidly, as if contemplating a trick. Neil led Emi to a pyramid made from truck tires, the kind that Emi had never been able to climb as a child, due to the hot odor of rubber and the way it had leaked into her palms. As they crawled inside, she found the smell of the rubber to be less potent, was worried instead by frequent breezes that stirred up the alleyway odors, and, without the direct sunlight to warm them, the cold. Neil placed an arm around her, while his other hand found the hem of her shirt, her stomach, the tight band of her bra, which stopped his progress momentarily. They could see the wheels of the boy's bicycle, as it appeared in one circle of light and then the next and then disappeared. The tip of Neil's tongue was in her ear, dipping into that grooved space that, from Emi's perspective, seemed to lose all sense of depth; the tongue might as well have been inside her brain. She did not know where her boyfriend had got such an idea, but she liked that he knew how to keep himself busy. It was an important quality. His teeth came down onto her earlobe. Then stopped. There was a whisper. "Is it happening?"

Both his hands inside her bra now, grabbing, pinching.

"Is it happening?" Neil's eyes were fixed on her. "Are you dissociating?"

Emi didn't understand the question, thought at first that he was asking if she had orgasmed and had no idea where to begin in her explanation of how such a thing would be accomplished. A certain book came to mind that her mother had given to her when she was nine. It was titled *How to Prepare for Your Womanly Body*, which she had thought was poorly worded and had shelved, reluctantly, next to a book called *Your New Guinea Pig*.

A face appeared in one of the tire circles then. It was the boy, off his bicycle now.

"You guys got any gum?" he asked them, oblivious to what he had interrupted.

They shook their heads.

"Me neither," he said, then opened his mouth to reveal a pulpy green ball on the flat of his tongue. "I'm just pretending that this old grape skin is gum." The boy disappeared again.

Neil, who seemed to have forgotten his question, blew on his hands, so that they would be warmer for pinching, Emi supposed. She was relieved when they were interrupted again, not by the boy, but by a voice from outside.

"Boss!" it cried. "Come home!"

Emi ducked away from Neil and crawled through the closest tire, back into the sunlight. She brushed the gravel from her knees and walked toward the swing set, where Maxie was teetering on the center swing, kicking her legs beneath her. Emi noticed how underdressed she was, the goose bumps visible across her bare arms. How truly old she looked without her lipstick.

"Let's find someplace else." Neil had appeared from the tire pyramid. He tugged at Emi's sleeve. "Jim said we could use his basement if we were desperate." Emi turned to him, interested in this new admission to desperation, wanting to find the evidence in his face. It looked the same as always: hungry, yellowish. She leaned in to kiss him, but he flinched.

"What?" she said. "I thought you liked being watched."

Neil's eyes flashed at Maxie, then back to Emi. He shook his head. "Gross," he said, and Emi understood. "Come on, let's get out of here."

The sun was low, behind them now, reflected gold by the windows of a small brick factory behind the park fence. This last flare of light, Emi noticed, made the smokestacks look more solid. Chiseled, as if into the sky. Another breeze blew up, scattering leaves. Maxie shivered on her swing and Emi wished that she could go to her, drape her sweater over those fleshy, goose-pimpled shoulders, tell her that Boss was coming home.

"I know her" was all that Emi could say, although it wasn't exactly true. She stepped away, squinting into the hard light, the bricks. She was thinking about Catherine. Catherine had been good enough to hold Emi's hand that day, as they walked from Mr. Albus's classroom to the nurse—the nurse who would not have the words for what had happened, who would, seeing Emi's tears, ask, again and again, which one of them was pregnant.

If they had ever held hands in their life, they could not remember and so had no experience when it came to letting go, once their hands became hot and uncomfortable. Catherine and Emi made it to the nurse's office this way, holding fast, not because they were friends, but because they were stubborn and liked to prove people wrong. They liked hard work. They had once built a boat from three inner tubes, two snow shovels, and the contents of a scrap pile, and had kept it afloat against the odds.

If Tooth *Could Mean* Heart

◆

When the pain in Helen's stomach began, her parents were concerned. They drove her to the emergency room, where the doctors could find nothing wrong. "Pain is common in pregnancy," they told her in apologetic, disparaging tones. But just to be safe, Helen was ordered an ultrasound. In a dark room, on a swimming, silvery screen, she was shown the parts of her baby. A thigh bone, a kidney, the fish mouth of the heart. The baby slipped in and out of the shadows, as if trying to keep its face above water. A drowning, living thing.

"Your baby is healthy," the obstetrician said, as if that solved it. So Helen went to her primary care doctor. She told him about the pain in her stomach, how it woke her at night, coming and going in strange, debilitating spells. It wasn't like a knife, as she had heard people describe excruciating pain, but rather a rebuke, a rogue part of her. The doctor took this news unceremoniously.

"Some women experience pain differently than others," he told her. He put his glasses back on and studied her form. By then, she was large, carrying the child far out in front, like a lengthwise watermelon. She often felt embarrassed by this, as if her stomach were somehow indecent, with its brown stripe, the creeping hairs. As if she could not just be modestly pregnant like every other woman. She hated how the lower part of her stomach plunged through the elastic band on her pants, drooping, like a cabbage hanging out of a grocery bag. And now, with this pain—pain itself, she was beginning to understand, was not good enough. You could not call a doctor's office and say, "I have pain." You had to be specific. It seemed that doctors were waiting for something very specific, the red flag that only they had the training to recognize. Helen knew of a famous playwright who had died of a heart attack. His only symptom had been a severe toothache. He had been following his wife to the car, on his way to the dentist, when he fell down dead. It seemed to Helen that if *tooth* could mean *heart*, then perhaps she needed to change her strategy.

"My ears are killing me," she told the doctor.

This was not working.

She had developed a somewhat embarrassing way to cope with the spells. It worked in the middle of the night, when she was alone, soaked in sweat. "There now," she'd say, "it's not so bad. You'll be better in no time." It was a part of herself that she did not recognize, this cooing voice, this pitiful little person, like a very old woman trying to comfort a dead cat. "You're a good girl," she'd say. "Hush now."

She remembered, as a child, the first time she became conscious of her heartbeat, a vexed hammering in her neck. She had shut herself into the bathroom, sat on the closed toilet lid, and pressed her finger to it, as if staving off a flood. Up until that day, she had believed in her own anatomy in the same way she believed in the continents on the map, the same way she had pretended to understand the constellations in the sky: with an abstract obedience. The discovery of her heart—or rather the acknowledgment of it—was an uncomfortable surprise. It meant that she was full of pieces, just like everyone else.

◆

Her friend Eliza had two children already and so she knew about pain.

"That baby is going to have to come out," she said. "Things are only going to get worse."

Eliza's youngest son had been born on the toilet, two months too early. Her only warnings of labor had been a twinge that morning, in her thighs, which she had dismissed as soreness from her yoga class. Then, when the stomach pains began, she blamed the Indian food and settled into the bathroom with a book. The baby had had to be incubated, and they had been told to prepare for the worst. Helen had seen the photographs from this time, shots taken in black and white: a wrinkled toe, a little mushroom face beneath a hat. The photographer had captured the size of the baby's wrist by sliding his father's wedding band over it. Despite the worry, the long, sleepless hours in the NICU, Eliza seemed to embrace the celebrity it brought. The heroism of giving birth at home, of mistaking childbirth for a bowel movement. Not just anybody could do that.

◆

Helen had gotten herself in to see a specialist. She was led to an examining room and told to change into a very short paper gown, which, with the addition of her large belly, fit more like an oversized T-shirt. She sat for a long time, eyeing various long, invasive-looking instruments set up along the counter, feeling cold, apprehensive. The doctor came in. He was a white-haired man who sat on a low stool so that he was eye level to a part of the gown that fit the most awkwardly. He had a list of questions, he said, and he began to read, without looking up.

"Vomiting," he said, as if it were a very formal state-ment, like the beginning of a sermon. "Nausea," to which Helen answered, "No. Not since the first trimes-ter." At this the doctor glanced up and seemed to notice her situation for the first time, his eyebrows raised, like a doctor who is interested in looking at an especially good wound. He wanted to know if sexual intercourse had become painful.

"I'm single," Helen said. She felt like a troublesome student, compelled to give a disruptive although cor-rect answer. She thought about her ex-boyfriend, Ju-lian, about his wide, dewy eyes. The doctor wanted to know if Helen had any history of mental illness. Helen studied his face, as he looked at her over his glasses—a sharp, elderly look, like a professor about to speak his mind, candidly, before a classroom. But the doctor did not speak.

The day before, Eliza had invited her over, made her herbal tea that smelled like lawn clippings, and then offered to be her birth partner.

"It's not just hand-holding," she said. "You need someone who is going to be straight with you."

Eliza had just finished telling her the story of a woman who'd given birth in the elevator of the hospital.

"At least I didn't do that," Eliza had said, as if the woman's act had been disgraceful—and not only that, but less desirable than having a baby on the toilet. Helen had heard many of these stories from Eliza: a woman who had given birth in her pant leg, who had to have the material cut carefully away so that the baby—a sticky, pearish lump—could be extracted safely; or the fifty-year-old woman who thought that her growing belly was cancer. Eliza had become obsessed with these stories, with these dopey women, who could not figure out childbirth.

"It's going to hurt like hell," she said.

◆

Helen left her appointment with the specialist feeling dull and misunderstood. In the end, there had been no need for the paper gown. No tests were performed. The doctor had set his clipboard down and given her a number to call. A therapist, he told her, and for the first time he had looked at her kindly, lifted his hand as if to touch her belly, then pulled it back. He shook her hand. Outside, the air was cool, windy, smelling like melting snow and exhaust from the parking lot. Helen could hear the humming of the hospital, the distant whoosh of the highway. She walked toward the bus stop, pulling her sweater around her belly. The baby was moving with an abrupt, liquid pressure, both aggravated and sweet. She thought about how Julian had put his hands on her stomach, poked at her jeans between her legs in a childish display of curiosity and love. Julian was flawed, but he was also tiresomely earnest. If he were here, Helen thought, he would try his best to understand. He would do everything to understand.

She found Julian at his apartment, blinking in his doorway, as though he had just woken up. He seemed very mysterious, standing there without his shirt—not quite a stranger, but a newer version of himself, a gaunt maturity having overtaken him, it seemed, since she had last seen him. He invited her in with awkward formality and offered her a chair at the small kitchen table. She was about to speak, a rehearsed little speech about why she had left him and why she had come back, when the pain returned—that terrible, defiant throbbing in her gut. She slumped forward in her chair and felt Julian's arms around her, trying to hold her up.

"Hey," he was saying. "Hey now," like a quiet, grateful, bewildered admonition. As he held her, looked at her with his terrified eyes, Helen thought about the famous playwright and his toothache, how his wife had reported hearing a loud thud as she walked to the car.

Schematic

♦

The inside of Toby's head was lined with plaid and could be packed like a suitcase. It reminded Toby of the pattern inside Doug's hunting jacket, which Doug had grown too big for and given to Sammy. That was the second thing Toby put inside his suitcase head—the jacket that had been Doug's. The first thing was this: Gram.

Sometimes, when he and Gram were alone, she'd ask him to try to remember.

"Think, Toby," she'd say, "to back before they put you in your mama's belly."

Toby would search the soft plaid of his mind, pushing past the hunting jacket, past Doug's old truck sprouting weeds in the front yard, past the names of planets and teachers at school. If he did this long enough, he'd see a Christmas tree, covered in silver hair, rising in a dark room. He, or someone like him, would reach out to touch it and a hand would come down hard on his head. The house with the Christmas tree was different than the house where he lived with Gram and his brothers, now that his mother was gone. The color of the wood was different; there was the stuffy feeling of things having been the same forever—so he guessed it must be the place Gram was talking about.

"Was it beautiful?" Gram wanted to know, her eyes shaking with little dots. Toby could see the tree, filling all the space in his vision, nightmarishly tall.

"Yes," he said, and she would breathe out, shuddering. "That's heaven, Toby."

When the pinball machine showed up in the basement, Gram was already dead. She had died in the early morning, hours before Sammy got there to help her down the stairs. It was Sammy's job to help her from the chair to her bed at night and from her bed back to her chair in the morning.

It was Toby's job to open the door for the churchwoman, who came on Tuesday afternoons to help

Gram in the bath. After Gram fell asleep, back in her chair, the churchwoman would give Toby a loaf of bread and a jug of milk to take to the kitchen. As she was leaving, she would sometimes look down at Toby and say, "Next time I'll bring you something special." Toby would look at the churchwoman's bag when she came around again, but it was never more than the loaf of bread and jug of milk. Doug could suck down half a jug like that just walking through the door after work.

It was Doug's job to make sure a flashlight turned on when he touched it to a battery. A long line of flashlights came at him all day on a belt, flashing once then moving on. He said that at night, when he got home, he could still see the lights, turning on and off, which might have been why he couldn't stay away from the pinball machine in the basement.

Doug had found it out behind the arcade, wedged between the dumpsters. He said that you didn't find games like that anymore, now that they were all digitized, the sound effects just recordings, the bells inside not real bells.

◆

The pinball machine—Toby wasn't allowed to touch it—was as tall as a table. It looked like a wooden coffin, propped up on four metal legs, but the sides were stenciled orange and green to show that it was a game, that there was something to be won or lost. There were two parts to this game: a playing field, under glass, where the shiny ball bounced around, and an upright scoreboard. On the face of the scoreboard was an image of a buffalo, running from a slew of arrows, one already pinned to a red blot in its hide. Behind the arrows rode three naked men on horses, with long, flying braids and big white smiles, pitched forward in cartoon ecstasy.

"Where did you come from?" Doug's voice was greasy and older than it had ever been.

Toby had just come down the basement stairs. He'd been about to ask Doug why Sammy wasn't home yet but got distracted by the smiles on the faces of the naked men shooting arrows. They must have been painted on a pane of glass, because their faces would suddenly light up from behind, making those smiles even brighter.

Doug stood at the end of the machine, fingering a metal plunger that looked like a ball. He snapped it back and the machine erupted into musical bells and loud pops. Toby watched Doug's long middle finger work a button at the side, holding it down, then tapping it furiously. There was a drop, a repetitive pinging of mechanical spinning numbers, and Doug brought his fist down and ran his pelvis into the end of the machine.

"Go to the hiding place and get me my cigarettes, Toby."

Doug and Sammy kept a store of bottles and magazines in the toolshed, under a bale of hay. Gram would be upset if she knew Doug was smoking in the house, but Toby supposed it must not matter now that she was dead, even if it had only been since that morning. Still, he thought it was important to remember that Gram wouldn't like it, and to feel sorry inside—a thing to keep.

Outside, Toby looked away from the windshield of the crumpled truck, afraid of seeing a reflection, or worse: the empty spots where the glass was cracked. It was dusk and the corn was roaring. Some people might think of corn as quiet, like a vegetable patch or a hayfield, but Toby knew that when the stalks were tall, they could crash together, louder than your voice if you ever got lost out there.

Sammy's bike was not propped in its usual spot

against the porch railing. He must have been burying Gram, like he'd buried their dog, Little Man, after he died from eating rat poison. Toby didn't consider how Gram would have fit on the bicycle or whether there would be a funeral. That morning, he'd heard Sammy saying she'd been dead most of the night and that Toby couldn't miss any more school. Toby walked to meet the bus, wondering why Gram had spent the night dead rather than asleep, if she was going to spend it in bed anyway. At school, he assumed the teachers knew everything, that every grown-up must know, so he hadn't said a word about Gram being gone.

Now, it was almost night. In the toolshed, Toby saw the cat that liked to sit on the hay. He would have liked to make friends with that cat, but Little Man hated cats, which made Toby feel bad about being nice to one. Once, Little Man had jumped out a two-story window to chase a kitten in the corn. Toby liked to tell that story, about his dog flying through the air. When he told it, he saw it from below, looking up at the dog's spotted belly, even though he'd been the one to open the upstairs window. That was another secret tucked in his head—not the window part, but the part about remembering something from a different pair of eyes.

The toolshed smelled like cat piss and putrid straw. The cat made a harsh, vibrating sound, then disappeared into a black corner. Toby felt around in the space below the hay for the carton of cigarettes. He wanted to hurry back and take a better look at the pinball machine. Its being there hadn't settled with him, how it could just appear like that, with all those parts springing into action without so much as a sputter.

Toby liked when you could see the start of something all the way to the end. Gram had made wreaths to sell at the church fair every year. They weren't the kind you'd get at Christmas; these were made from bits of old clothes and ribbon and sometimes gold wire, or something special, like a charm in the shape of a horse. Toby liked to watch the wreaths grow under her hands, because he knew what to expect from the first knot to the end. Gram's old hands would claw up and down, braiding and pulling, like crows building a nest. Toby would watch her hands so he wouldn't have to see the dark windows of the living room that looked back at him with his own face.

Gram had meant for the wreaths to be sold as decorations for the home—some were pink and green for Easter, or soft and blue for a baby's room—but she found that most people liked to use them for graves, or markers on the side of the road. Toby's bus passed one every day, right around where Anne Tracy was dropped off. It was pink and red—the red coming from one of Toby's old shirts—with a big bow that always looked crumpled and wet. A girl who had been in Doug's class died when her truck had hit a tree. Doug said her body flew from the driver's seat twenty feet into the cow pasture and that, by the time the fire department showed up, the cows had licked off all her clothes.

"Cows are curious animals," Doug said. "They'd lick the paint off an army tank if you let them, just to try to figure it out." Doug was always telling that story, like it meant something important. Toby wondered why the wreath had been nailed to the tree and not put twenty feet into the cow pasture, but no one ever answered that question, so he'd focus on the red shirt. It had been his Christmas shirt, with a snowman on the front.

"There was a cat," Toby said when he handed the cigarettes to his brother. Doug pulled one with his teeth, grimacing. His face was red and orange in the glow of the machine.

"You know about Gram?" Doug asked with the cigarette still on his bottom lip. Toby nodded, looking at the smiling men with the flashing teeth. He wondered how Doug had gotten something as big and loud as that down into the cellar without anyone noticing. Toby had an uncomfortable feeling, like he was seeing someone's insides, open and aglow and full of strange pumping and flexing.

"Sammy took a job at the Hathaways' for a few days," Doug said. "When he gets back, tell him he'd better strip that bed down."

Sammy was always taking jobs at the Hathaways', or farther down the road—for Mr. Delaney when it was haying season. Mr. and Mrs. Hathaway liked Sammy, liked him so much, he bragged, that when he turned ten, Mr. Hathaway taught him how to drive the tractor, so he wouldn't have to push a wheelbarrow anymore. Some days, when the work was slow, Mrs. Hathaway would even call him in sick for school. Gram would never do a thing like that.

Doug jammed his hip into the pinball machine and the bells started. His fingers twitched over the buttons and smoke came trailing out his nose, like he was con-nected to a big engine.

Toby found a bag of chips in the kitchen and took them upstairs to his room where there was a TV. He turned it on so he wouldn't have to hear the popping bells and Doug's swearing downstairs. He turned the sound up so he wouldn't have to feel the door to Gram's room, which he hadn't had the courage to close.

In the morning, the TV was showing a commercial for a breakfast-making machine that could pop out scrambled eggs, or little, perfectly round pancakes. Toby looked at it a long time, wondering how long he'd been awake and why everyone in the commercial was shouting. There was something about their beaming faces that made him uneasy, so he turned the switch and went looking for Sammy, to get ready for school. He remembered the pinball machine halfway down the stairs, the same time as he heard the bells and the *ching-ching*s from below the floorboards.

Doug was always at the factory this time in the morning, unless it was Saturday, which in that case meant no school. If Sammy was at the Hathaways', then Gram would be waiting in bed for her orange juice. Toby went to the fridge and found the bottle. He shook it and poured it into one of Gram's plastic cups with the built-in straw. Even as he was walking back upstairs

with the juice in his hand, he knew what he was doing must be wrong. But he decided it was just a game,
something to be carried out from beginning to end. He
went into Gram's room, stood by the bed, and poured
the juice onto the pillow. Back downstairs, Doug was
tearing up the kitchen, drawers hanging open, papers
and bits of mail scattered everywhere, Doug swinging around like a scarecrow in high winds. He stopped
moving when he caught Toby standing in the doorway.
He blinked his slow, red eyes.

"What happened to school?" he said. The sun was
coming through the window, hard. Toby saw the patterns of dust and fingerprints along the countertops,
something that must have always been there, hiding
from sight.

"I thought we could make pancakes," Toby said,
not knowing why he was saying it. "I thought we could
make them really round this time."

Doug's voice was like a drain clogged with hair, getting ready to burble something foul.

"Get your ass to school," he said.

Outside the wind was tearing through the corn-
stalks, and farther away, the neighbor's black cows stood
together, still as statues, because there were no flies to

swat and there was no fresh grass to eat. Toby ran past the truck and down the driveway, straight down the road—not so much from Doug, but from the pinball machine. There was no way Doug could carry a thing like that. He'd need a truck to move it to the house. Toby remembered the night Doug rolled home with the truck all smashed up. Gram had been madder than ever.

"I want you to look at my face, Douglas!" she yelled. "I want you to see me when I say I will be dead before this family can afford a new truck."

And now she was and there was no new truck, just that loud, flashing mess in the basement, like it had always been there, waiting for someone to turn it on.

Toby meant to take the road down to the Hathaways' farm. They had big horses there with feathery legs that turned to icicles in the winter. Sometimes, when school was closed, Sammy would take Toby with him, letting him break the ice on the water troughs with a hammer. But when he came to the fork, Toby found himself walking his bus route instead, unable to deviate from the course he was used to taking day after day.

He made it to the shoulder of the highway before he heard the slow crunch of a car pulling up behind him, then quick footsteps over gravel.

"What on earth brought you out here?" A gloved hand grabbed his shoulder and he was strapped quickly into the front seat of the churchwoman's station wagon, a photo album wedged under his bottom. The woman got behind the wheel and struggled with a pile of keys in her lap, shaking her head. Her lips peeled back over her teeth in a way that made Toby think she was looking to bite someone. She was muttering.

"No coat," she said to her lap, then turned the key in the ignition. She was wearing a purple windbreaker zipped halfway over a sweater with an embroidered turkey on the front. Toby noticed his fingers were red and stiff. The vents blew lukewarm air at him.

"I'm sorry to hear about your grandma," the churchwoman said. "But it's always best for folks to pass on before winter hits."

The back seat of the station wagon was stacked with paper towels, bags of dog food, plastic grocery bags bulging with scarves and mittens. The woman's hand came down on his knee.

"She's in heaven now," she said.

Toby pictured the big tree, covered in silver hair, taking up all his vision. The hand coming down from nowhere. He rubbed his forehead as if he'd been struck and wondered where there was room for Gram in that heaven, if maybe she'd have to find herself another one. As they pulled away from the curb, the woman asked questions about school, about Toby's mother. It had been a long time since Toby had seen his mom. He tried to keep her face packed safely away, but whenever he looked for it, he could only come up with the face of Ms. Stevens, his teacher from last year. He thought about sleeping and dreaming and being dead—how, if you couldn't do all three at once, maybe you could do two. Which two, then? He rearranged the possibilities in his head until everything felt pushed around.

Toby woke in his driveway, the car idling, but the churchwoman was no longer behind the wheel. The station wagon was parked close to Doug's old truck and Toby could just see the rim of the truck's window. Something solid seemed to roll over inside, and Toby covered his eyes with his hands. The vents blew hot air, rough against his face. When he opened his fingers, the churchwoman was coming down the porch steps, show-ing her teeth, like she was going to nip. Doug was in the doorway, smoking and waving angrily. He was holding some sheets of paper in one hand, and he stopped waving to look at them as soon as the woman was off his porch.

Toby's door swung open and he slid off the photo album, into the cold. He watched the churchwoman's station wagon nudge back, then creep forward to turn around before creaking away. Toby felt as though he'd been gone all day. His stomach growled, and something meowed inside the old truck. The screen door of the house bounced and when Toby looked back, Doug was gone.

That was when the boy showed up on Sammy's bike. Toby thought it was Sammy at first, but his brother had reddish hair and a white line under his chin from when he cut himself jumping off the statue in front of their school. This boy had brown hair, no scar, and a tooth missing at the bottom, just like Toby. The boy jumped off the bike, letting it drop at the side of the house, then walked up the porch steps and caught the bouncing door in his hand. He was wearing Sammy's hunting jacket—the one that used to be Doug's.

Toby wondered if it wasn't Sammy after all, if Sammy wasn't playing a joke on him.

"Hey," Toby said, "you're supposed to clean up the bed upstairs."

The boy paused, still holding the door, as if he was trying to hear something far away. The hunting jacket looked a little long on him and Toby noticed the tear in the pocket, where Doug had caught it on a fence crossing the train tracks. There was no question that it was the same jacket. Toby tried again: "If you want dinner, you're going to have to talk to Doug about it."

But the boy didn't say anything. He just went inside.

When Toby got to the basement, the boy was already there with Doug. The two of them were sitting on an old mattress that had been dragged close to the pinball machine, which was still blinking silently. It was clear to Toby, now that they were indoors, that the boy was not Sammy. He swallowed. He felt the truth of it in his throat, the way crying sometimes comes before pain, before his brain understood what he was seeing. The boy sitting on the mattress looked just like him. He had the same hair, the same face. He looked exactly like Toby. Toby could not speak, or make a sound, so he stood at the bottom of the basement stairs and watched them.

Doug showed the boy something on the piece of paper, his voice soft, patient, like Toby remembered from a long time ago. He wondered if Doug was sleeping down there now.

"Here's where the trouble is," Doug said, pointing to the paper. "The ball hits the spinner and the wrong lights light up."

The Toby on the mattress paid close attention to whatever was on the paper, and the Toby standing at the bottom of the stairs was looking at him. He couldn't explain what was happening, only that Gram was gone and if she could just leave like that, then maybe people could also just show up.

Doug handed the piece of paper to the boy and went to the pinball machine, pulling back the trigger and ramming his hip into the corner. The machine flashed and popped. It seemed much louder than the night before. Doug's face swam in the orange and red lights.

"See? The wrong fucking lights. On and off. All over the playing field."

A white smile sprung up under his nose, like the smiling men chasing the buffalo. It reminded Toby of a dog that couldn't properly close its mouth.

Toby went to his room and turned on the TV. He watched it until the room grew dark and the five thirty news came on. He could never follow the words spoken on the news, the way each sentence rolled into the next, like waves that never broke. Toby had a box of Gram's fruit candies and chewed in a daze, until he heard footsteps in the hall. It was the other Toby. He came into the room and sat on the floor, breathing softly through his mouth.

"It's called a scheme-attic," the other Toby said, sliding over the piece of paper. It looked like a tangle of black lines and circles, with numbers scattered around, like an impossible connect-the-dots puzzle.

"I took it from him," he said. He grabbed the paper back and left the room.

Toby went to the window, pushing his face to the glass so that his own reflection would not be in the way. He saw the other Toby cross the front yard to Doug's truck, pull open the driver's door with some difficulty, then climb inside. The truck door closed and Toby had a dark feeling in his chest, like something had crawled in there and turned to stone.

The churchwoman was there the next morning, clunking her shoes around downstairs. Toby found her running water over a heap of dirty dishes in the sink. There was a long gurgle that seemed to reach somewhere deep into the house. The woman looked up and wrinkled her nose at Toby, tightening her lips, but then she seemed to remember something pleasant and her face changed. She turned off the water and the two of them stood, hearing the faint pinging of pinball from below.

"Good morning, Toby," the woman said, smiling. Her eyes fell onto the boots on his feet, which he'd slept in.

"Why don't you come with me? I have something special for you in the car." The woman took his hand and began walking. They made it to the front porch and Toby saw the station wagon parked next to the old truck, just like it had been the day before. Her grip tightened and he was suddenly afraid: What if the other Toby was still in the cab? What if he was asleep, or watching from the window?

Toby could not decide which would be worse. The other Toby shouldn't be there. Not in Doug's truck. Not with Sammy's jacket. Toby pulled his hand away, scratching his palm on the churchwoman's ring. A wind started to blow and the corn jumped in waves, making a coarse sound. He stepped down from the porch and heard the woman say his name in a low, warning tone, as if she knew what he was thinking. He tried another step forward, almost surprised at the working of his own free will, and he ran.

Toby could feel the other Toby watching, sitting cold behind the wheel of the truck. He could see himself, through the eyes of the other Toby, disappearing into the corn, followed by the churchwoman, who lunged repeatedly after the hood of his sweater, like reaching for the leash of a runaway dog. It was easy for him to run through the straight rows of corn, dodging into another row whenever he felt the churchwoman getting too close. But after some time, he slowed and realized that the sound he was running from was not the woman's breath, or the swish of her windbreaker, but the stalks crashing together behind him. He stood still for a long time, unable to think of what to do. There were spaces between the rows of stalks, like long, narrow avenues. You might expect to be able to see straight down them, all the way to the end of the field, but it didn't work that way. To Toby, it felt like trying to remember too far back in time and just seeing the same memories over and over. He crouched down, close to the bases of the stalks, and saw the tracks left by field mice, how precise the little toes were on every print. He liked this better than trying to find his way out.

He'd been lost in the corn before, times when he'd gone in after Sammy, trying not to be seen, but also trying not to lose sight of his brother. One time, Toby followed Sammy and watched him sit on the damp, clay-like dirt. Watched him take from his pocket a book of matches, strike them, one after another, until all the matches were burned. Sammy had left the black burnt-up matches in the dirt, but he put the empty book back in his hunting jacket, the hunting jacket that Toby was supposed to get one day, when he was old enough to carry a rifle, and his arms were long enough to not get lost inside the sleeves. When he could look down the length of it and button all the buttons, from top to bottom, without having to stop and start over. Without having to ask for help.

A Bone for Christmas

◆

An old woman had not left her house for a very long time. She had missed dentist appointments and a meeting with the podiatrist. It was possible that her son was keeping her inside the house against her will, selling her belongings, neglecting her care. The girl who had reported the case had not wanted to identify herself. She did, however, have much to say about the issue of cat feces.

Everywhere, she had said over the phone, and her voice had cracked with emotion. It's like a minefield. Of cat shit. Petra, ever diligent, had written this in the file.

The old woman's house was on the mountain, on a road called Bottom Furnace. It was late January, so there was ice on the mountain also, and frost heaves, and some small, impassable bridges. There was never cell service. Petra kept a flashlight and a blanket in the trunk of her car along with a set of flannel underwear, still in the package. She had never asked herself how, in the case of a breakdown, she would get herself into the underwear.

Petra liked street names, how strange they could sometimes be. Bottom Furnace, she imagined, would go well with Lost Lake Road and Swearing Hill. Last week, she had driven to a house on Mad Tom and to another on a road called Twitchel. She liked the old names of the people that she visited: the Ethels and the Hirams. Hyacinth and Sissy and Eugenia. Lester, with his pipe and his large, scaly ears. She made sure that they were being cared for, that they had enough fuel for the winter, and sometimes, out of kindness, she checked the mousetraps for them. She asked if there was anyone harming them, or if any of their medication had gone missing.

There was wildlife too: the black bears, the folded flight of herons over her windshield. How red foxes trotted with their heads turned, conscious of traffic. In the winter, there were mostly little birds, crows cawing, and recently, a small white cat in her backyard. She had built a shelter for it from a Styrofoam cooler lined with straw, after seeing the design in a children's magazine.

Can we let her inside? Petra's son had asked about the cat, his concern only deepening a well of desire within her to let worlds mingle, just for once.

Petra turned onto the mountain road. She removed a glove, finger by finger, with her teeth and placed her hand against the heating vent on the dashboard. The radio station had been playing Brahms all morning, which always brought her heart to a crawl, made her feel like damaged goods—in an appreciative sense. It carried a memory too, something almost a decade gone: a mansion, august with green vines and piano attics. Walking there under the weight of her violin case, over a footbridge where there was a pond, reflecting the colors of dawn. How young she had been, feeling as though she were truly, truly herself, in the same way an adolescent moose charges top-heavy from the tree line. Endearing; terrifying.

There had been an ice storm the previous week and some of the trees along the road were bowed or broken. She could see the fresh wood where someone had used a chainsaw to clear a limb that had fallen. The wood chips were bright against the gray, muddied snow. Lately, the majority of her cases had taken place on these remote stretches, in areas referred to as *hollows*—places that seemed to Petra to be utterly random and lonely. It worried Petra's husband to know that his wife was out there, by herself. For his sake, she often left out certain details, like her encounters with unchained dogs, or the old man in the wheelchair, who had snorted a line of cocaine off the back of his gnarled hand. And, of course, there were things like cat feces, which, knowing her husband, would have dismayed him most of all.

Her husband was a tortured man. He would not use public restrooms, or see movies at the theater. Sometimes he microwaved slices of bread, or pickles, of all things. Sometimes he boiled water before drinking it, just to make himself feel better. After six years of marriage, he had never shared a drink with his wife, never sampled food from her plate, never used the shower after her without first wiping it down.

Yes, he'd say, with perfect self-awareness. I know that it's all in my head.

◆

She found the address without difficulty, just as the intermezzo on the radio was ending. The house was lopsided with a mossy roof and an enclosed front porch almost fully obscured by blinds. She could see, from where the blinds were askew, that the porch was filled with bits of furniture with the legs thrown upward, sunbleached fabrics, and piles of newspapers with the pages bent against the glass.

Caroline Marrows was the old woman's name. Petra confirmed the spelling on the case folder, then repeated it under her breath as she walked over the ice to the house.

If I don't do it—repeat it like that—she had tried to explain to her husband, then I will spend the whole interview worrying that I've said the wrong name. Like a madness.

You mean an idiosyncrasy, he had replied.

A girl in short sleeves and a winter hat met Petra at the inner door. She seemed to look beyond her, through one of the cracks in the blinds, as if checking to see what kind of car she had arrived in, or if there was anyone else with her.

Petra extended her hand.

I'm here to see Mrs. Marrows, she said. The girl

did not speak, but she moved aside for Petra to pass through. Her face was long and peevish. She reminded Petra of someone working at a carnival, a face that says, *Come on and try your luck.*

Petra entered a cluttered kitchen with a warped linoleum floor. Above the sink, which was piled with dishes, there was a small window with a drawn curtain. The hard winter light glowed through a pattern of red flowers flecked in the center with yellow. Petra found herself taken by these curtains, their implied intentions: like a petition for all that was nice and long ago.

She was accustomed to finding her way through unfamiliar houses. Upstairs, they would sometimes tell her. Casey's old room, as if she were privy to the house's history. Once, she'd walked into a log cabin and was led by a German shepherd to a skylit room where a large woman lay suspended in a hammock. The whole space was rigged with hammocks, for the cats and ferrets, for potted plants by the window. The woman was on oxygen and had a list of health issues. She told Petra that she was saving her money for a trained monkey that could change out the toilet paper, fetch chips with nimble hands that would not crush the bag. A ferret had emerged from inside the woman's sleeve then tumbled to the floor, limping away to some other, unimaginable part of the house.

What Petra remembered vividly was the floor, which was, due to the hammocks, almost completely bare—or at least would have been, had it not been for the tumbleweeds of dust, fur, and little pellets of dry food, compressed so densely that the cats batted them around like toys. Petra had stared at this expanse of oddly sculptural bits of filth and thought, sadly, of her husband. How the sight would have overwhelmed his mind, propelled him into a fit of highly specific madness, like the time he took sandpaper to his top lip, because he was convinced that it would prevent him from catching a cold. She had given him two Xanax and sent him to bed. The result had been so effective that she often wondered if she could get away with spiking his coffee some mornings.

It would shed no light on her husband's condition to reveal that he spent most of his days working with dirt. In his lab, he dealt mostly with a black, pungent substance called char, which needed to be stirred and measured. His work was environmental, a tireless search for what

was fertile, what dark, smelly matter would best pro-
duce life. He moved about the counters and test tubes
with his horn-rimmed glasses, his long lab coat and nice
shoes, barely touching anything.

He dislikes correspondences by mail, his assistant
said. Make sure you never lick the envelope.

And then the baby was born. He was born gaunt and
nearly translucent. The infant's frailty was something
that the man in horn-rimmed glasses could understand,
wholly, he found, and he kept vigil in the NICU with
such haggard tenderness that Petra was spun right up
with it. She joined him in his delirium: the cleaning
of little red skin folds, hot towels from the dryer, and
bottle temperatures. Visitors were asked to speak at a
low volume and douse their hands in disinfectant lotion.

Petra found Mrs. Marrows in a back room where the
windows, curtains and all, were cocooned in sheets of
plastic. They billowed every few minutes in the draft,
which gave her the disorienting feeling of being on a
ship, or very high off the ground. Besides the peevish
girl who had met her in the doorway, there had also
been a man, presumably the old woman's son, who had

not spoken, but nodded to the side, so that Petra was not sure if he was acknowledging her or cracking his neck. He was wearing a hooded sweatshirt, the front of which was obscured, almost down to his belt buckle, by a thin beard. He had taken a step back to allow Petra to pass through to the hallway, and she had heard the linoleum pop and groan beneath his steel-toe boots.

Mrs. Marrows smiled from her armchair. The way that she was seated there, beneath a heap of afghans, reminded Petra, eerily, of a trick of puppetry, as if the woman were standing behind the chair, sticking her head through a hole.

Mrs. Marrows, Petra began, worried momentarily that she had the wrong name. I hope you are staying warm.

The woman nodded. The plastic on the windows made a sucking sound, and Petra once again had the sensation of being in a tower, high above the ground. She noticed that the room was almost bare. It might have passed for tidy had it not been for the whorls of cat hair pressed into the rug, like the meteorological images of clouds.

◆

Last spring she had brought her husband to a concert. She had not told him that she knew the composer, that once, in college, they had slept together. The music was tremulous and experimental. She was filled with visions of the deep sea, of dazzling ancient creatures.

It was the first time that they had left their son at home with a babysitter. He had just reached the age that her friends had warned her about. It will be *why* this and *why* that, they told Petra. Just you wait. But her son rarely asked why. Instead, his questions were fully formed, with their own gravity.

How do you know that a caterpillar is not cut in half?

Who *is* a window washer, really?

After the concert, Petra's husband had frowned. Too long, he said. It sounded like listening to someone weeping. For too long.

The boy was asleep when they got home, the babysitter watching television with her bare feet on the couch cushion. Everything was fine, she said, except he would not eat his beets. He was worried that they would stain his teeth forever. He thought that the celery would tie a knot in his stomach. She shrugged.

Petra's husband had smiled at the babysitter as he counted her bills at the door, but then he spent the rest of the night scrubbing the couch cushion, turning it around and forgetting which was the sullied side, then cleaning the rest of the house, just in case. Petra could hear him going through the silverware as she fell asleep, hearing music in her dreams, like the clink of polished knives laid out across the table.

Something was wrong. The man with the long beard and the steel-toe boots was not happy. He had appeared in the doorway, his head stooped. I'm just not comfortable, he was saying. I'm just not comfortable with her being here.

When he stretched his arms up to grab the doorframe, Petra saw the hair on his belly. She saw his belt buckle, the butt of a smallish gun just off-center. I'm just not comfortable.

The plastic on the windows billowed. Petra did not know if the man had meant to reveal the gun as a threat, or if it had truly been an accident. She had a strong desire to be back in her car, to have her public radio, her fingers jammed into the warm vents. I must not act rashly, she thought, followed by: If I could only rip through the plastic, I might escape through the window.

The man looked at her.

I have an uncomfortable feeling about her, he said, still not addressing Petra outright, although he did not appear to be speaking to the old woman in the chair either. It heightened her sense of danger, to be disregarded this way, as one would a prisoner. She looked down, avoiding his eye, and noticed that her hand was on the zipper of her purse. Somehow, she had unzipped it, perhaps in an unconscious effort to reach for her pepper spray. Her husband bought her a new can of it every Christmas. He said that you never knew how much potency was lost over time.

It doesn't spray as fast as you expect it to, he would explain, year after year. You have to keep your finger down. It was useful advice.

As her son grew, his questions continued: What if an acorn fell into his mouth while he was yawning? If a finger grew too long? Just yesterday, he had sat behind her in the car and spoken of next Christmas—the child only ever talked about next Christmas, as if the present or approaching Christmas was too real to bear. He wanted to have a tree strung with popcorn and bells. But not stars. Never stars.

Do glass planets exist? he asked. Do children ever get a bone for Christmas? Just a bone?

What's your name? the man asked Petra. She told him and he shook his head, unconvinced. I'm not comfortable with you being here anymore, he told her, his index finger pointing to the floor. With the other hand, he adjusted his belt.

They should all just sit down and talk, thought Petra, but the only piece of furniture was the old woman's chair. In the corner, there was a large crater in the rug where something round and heavy once stood—the base of a lamp, maybe, or some kind of barrel. As Petra's eyes traveled over the rug, she saw many other shapes: small circles from a set of table legs, the right angles of a chest or bookshelf, all of which made her feel as if the world were disappearing around her, piece by piece. She took a step forward and the man stood rigid, blocking her path.

She had seen her husband angry plenty of times. The way he moved his tongue around inside his mouth, as if tasting his own fury. How he studied his knuckles, wondering, she supposed, if this was the day that they would burst at the seams. But perhaps she was not being fair, for he had never been violent. With their son he was always soft-spoken. But one night they had gone out with friends and she had become quite drunk, grabbing hold of him for balance, touching him flirtatiously—her own husband—so that the other couple raised their eyebrows in amusement. At home, he could not look at her.

You embarrassed yourself, he said, and she saw there, in the line of his jaw, all the capacity any man had ever had for hatred.

The man blocking Petra's path did not seem to know what to do with his hands. They hung stiffly at his sides and it made Petra feel a little sorry for him, as if he could not commit to being fully menacing. This did not mean that Petra was unafraid; his indecisiveness signaled to her that he was capable of anything. When she had arrived in the room, she had noticed an aged brass pole in the corner to her left. Her first thought was that it was some kind of antique pole for an IV bag, used for a homebound patient. Medical equipment—albeit never outdated medical equipment—was not an uncommon sight in her work. But it was not an IV pole. Petra saw now that it was a stand with a curled hook meant to hang a birdcage. At some time, perhaps in the distant past, or perhaps not so long ago, someone had kept a bird and fed it food and talked to it through the bars. Petra's son would have something to say about this. It occurred to her that she might try telling the man that she had a son, that her son was waiting for her to come home. He was the kind of boy who would worry about the moss on the roof, wonder if the lacy white roots dangled down from the ceiling. He would not like there to be a stand without a cage.

The girl who had opened the door for Petra appeared behind the man. The man's shoulders softened. He scratched the inside of his ear with his pinkie. Whatever he had wanted to do, it seemed, he could not do in front of her.

Come with me, he said, and he motioned for Petra to follow.

Once, during one of her investigations, Petra had discovered a dead body. She had been obliged to wait around for the state's attorney and the medical examiner to show up. She had had to pee, but she did not want to be in the bathroom when they arrived. She did not even know if it was permissible to use the toilet of the deceased. The body was that of an old man, who had seemed to have fallen and caved in one side of his head. There had been no odor until the body was moved and the wound, which had been pressed into the floor, was exposed. When she got home, she had gone straight to the shower, turned the heat up as high as she could stand it. She wondered, briefly, as she scrubbed beneath her fingernails, if this was how her husband felt all the time, this itch, this dread. It's not about dirt, she had thought, but the epiphany had not lasted, and the next day, she had found herself stupefied once again, when he threw into the waste bin a perfectly good carton of milk.

Petra's husband did love her. He loved his lab and his nice shoes. He loved the deep freeze of winter. It was a relief to make his own heat, he said, to know that it was his own. He loathed the ocean for its warm currents and the city for its hot breath, all the secondhand air. Where there was life and where there was passion, there was also filth, he said. And when it came to sex, he braced himself against his wife, like a tree trunk in a flood, waiting for her desire to run its course.

With the composer it had been different. They had met in a student ensemble in that grand music building with the vines. He had played first violin and she, second. The composer had been a child prodigy. He could play twenty instruments by the time he was fifteen. Petra could not even name twenty instruments. She was always impressed when she remembered the name for the timpani, that thunderous one.

The composer had been sloppy, kissing her all over, like a house painter without a plan. His arms were just strong enough that he found he could lift her, although he couldn't figure out where to put her. He swept the books off his desk and they landed facedown on the floor. She remembered being flattered, as if she had not expected to be revered over books, especially by someone so studious. She knew, even back then, that he was brilliant. She had watched him play, his bow drawing the notes from the strings, each measure a new tension discovered, then broken. But then there he was, wheezing and sweating, bumping his elbow, pulling her hair.

I like this, she had wanted to say. But the composer seemed ashamed.

I have a lot on my mind, he told her and picked up her clothes from around the room.

◆

They had moved into the kitchen. The girl in the winter hat had made herself comfortable, sitting at the table across from Petra and lighting a cigarette. In front of her was a clutter of bottles, paper plates, various greasy tools that did not seem to belong. From beneath the mess, she unearthed a fashion magazine and began to read it, turning the pages with the hand that held the cigarette, decadently, completely at ease. The man with the long beard stood beside Petra's chair. He had said nothing of the gun and Petra was beginning to wonder if she had been mistaken. Maybe her eyes had deceived her and she had been following his orders for nothing.

I love my mother, the man said to her. Something bulged in his jaw.

Petra felt sympathy for the man and so did not know what led her to say what she said next. She leaned back in her chair.

I was told there would be cat feces, she said.

The man looked at her. His beard, Petra noticed, was graying near his mouth and chin, but down at the bottom, where it was sparser, she could see the bright orange hairs, glowing in the sun.

She clasped her hands together. Cat excrement, she said.

The man grew rigid, looked at the girl in the winter hat, who lowered her eyes and flipped her magazine, suggesting that she did not intend to hear any of this.

He turned back to Petra.

What? he asked her. *What* did you say?

Your house, she said, louder this time. It's not as filthy as I expected.

Sometimes Petra dreamed of the composer. She dreamed of his lips pressed all over her, his hands grabbing. There was something about her that he could not figure out, and he would become more and more enraged, moving her around the room, forcing her against the wall until the plaster cracked. And sometimes, because it was a dream, it became her skin that was cracked and then her whole body, under the force of him. Parts of her came right off, like bits of glass, and, in the midst of her arousal, which was strongest in this dream, there would be a small voice crying out, as if to a child. Stay off the floor! You'll cut your feet!

◆

The man leaned in. His beard intersected a ray of sunlight from the window, which, catching the lighter strands, illuminated the whole, ragged length of it. Something near his waist clunked against the edge of the table.

Who called you? he asked. He seemed rejuvenated by this new, palpable offense. Petra could smell his breath. It smelled like a hole, like wet tobacco, like menthol.

I have no idea, she said.

Roland, said the girl in the hat. Roland, she said again in a scolding voice that was older and huskier than Petra would have expected. But he paid no attention and reached again for his belt.

Petra wondered if the man would really keep a loaded gun pointing down his pants, if he would wave it around, like a lunatic in a movie, or aim it straight. She wondered why she had not tried to run, or why she even bothered carrying the pepper spray. You have to hold down the button, she thought. It doesn't come out like you think.

Roland, said Petra, just as the girl had. What a big name to have, she thought, way up here on this mountain. She looked at him and found that she was laughing. She said his name again—Roland!—laughing harder still, just to see what he would do.

Sometimes, Petra passed cows standing coolly on the wrong side of the fence. Roadkill that had been rained on and was hard to identify. A raccoon, circling in a daze under the midday sun. Her husband liked raccoons, because they washed their food.

They also eat trash, she explained.

Her son worried that raccoons might not recognize their own reflections. Because of their masks.

Last summer, a rabbit had darted in front of Petra's car. It would have been killed by the pickup truck in the oncoming lane had the truck not stopped abruptly as well. There was a man behind the wheel of the truck. He had a pipe in his mouth. The rabbit cowered in the space just in front of the truck's tire and Petra met the man's eye. She shook her head, as if to say, *Don't go.* He held onto the pipe and nodded and they both waited. At some point, the rabbit had hopped back toward Petra's car and disappeared from view. The man in the truck shrugged: the rabbit could be anywhere. So they waited some more.

Go, Mommy, Petra's son had said from the car seat. He wanted to know about ghosts. He wanted to know where green olives came from.

Petra's husband often wanted to know how long she spent in the shower after work. Did she remember to wash her hands when she was in there? And her feet? Letting the water run over them was not the same as washing. Getting dirty was not proof that she was helping anybody.

Go, Mommy, said the boy. Petra had looked once more at the man in the truck and then stepped on the gas, leaving the rabbit—dead or alive—behind.

What if a house painter paints all the doors shut? her son had asked.

Petra had driven on.

What about pitchforks? Bathtub drains? Do storks ever forget how to walk? They passed a cornfield, a country store. Someone was hammering a PICK YOUR OWN BLUEBERRIES sign onto a post. Petra pulled the car over and turned off the engine.

Look, she said, turning to the boy. One day I will die and a bunch of men that you don't know will dig a deep hole. They will put me in the hole and I will stay there until I am a pile of bones. Any questions?

The boy stared at her and shook his head. He looked out the window at the person hammering the sign: a woman wearing an apron over a long patterned dress. He was silent as his mother started the car and turned back onto the road. It seemed to him that they drove for a long time, until the passing telephone wires created a sort of wave, a pulsing nothingness in his head. And when they reached home, he saw that his house was standing where they had left it, that it had not floated away. He saw his father's face in the window, exhausted from holding it down.

Farmer, Angel

◆

If Angel heard about what Beth did to the horses, she would nod her head, as if she had always expected it to happen and here it was. She believed everything, mutely, with the callous faith of the chronically exhausted. She would chalk it up to the horses' good temperament. Had she told Beth about the time Big Red got himself tangled in a bunch of fence ribbon? He had been only a colt and he'd had the good sense to stand there without moving until someone came to his rescue.

"Standing there, wrapped in twenty feet of fence up to his hocks," she'd beamed. "The best and the brightest."

◆

Beth had woken early that morning in her cabin below the barn. The sun had not yet risen, but there was a silver infiltration of light coming in from the window, making the interior of the cabin seem strangely uniform, like opening your eyes underwater. It was a single rectangular room with a door at one end and a miniature woodstove at the other. There were no shelves. No table. Beth's folded laundry, her toiletries, and books were lined up against the wall, leaving only a thin strip of floor between her belongings and the bunk. Her bra hung from a hook by the window. All she had to do was reach for it and she could get dressed right there in bed.

Outside, the mist had not risen and everything beyond it—the pastures, the mountains—appeared gray and purple. The cats were sitting in front of the farmhouse door, tongues smoothing lines across their fur, the pink pads of their feet skyward. Beth clucked at them and they paused, their green eyes brightening. She began up the hill, passing the water pump, the stack of plastic buckets waiting to be scrubbed. Birds swooped down from under the eaves of the barn and spider webs spanned new lengths across the farm equipment.

Inside the barn the odor of the horses was strong. They kicked their stalls and grunted. The mares

stretched their long back legs and lifted their tails, urinating a hole in their bedding. Beth walked up the long
aisle between the stalls to the feed room. She scooped
grain and poured it into the horses' feed buckets, tutting
at them to be patient, to keep their big heads out of her
way. While they ate, she sat on a hay bale, resting on
her elbows, and watched the sparrows in the rafters fly
back and forth. They settled, softening their feathers,
then jumped up, as if they were always sitting on pins.
Beth followed them with her eyes at first, until something seemed to shift. It was as if, instead of moving
of their own volition, the birds were now being pulled
across the air by her gaze. She looked right, the birds
traveled right. She looked left, they picked up and flew
back to where they had begun. It was a strange, child-
like notion.

It gave her an idea.

Beth walked up the center aisle of the barn and un-
latched the chains to each stall door. She walked slowly,
with her head down, focusing on the toes of her English
riding boots. When she got to the far end of the barn,
she turned around and saw that the aisle was filled with
horses. They made wide, milling circles. They backed
into each other, jumping and clattering their hooves

against the floor. Eyes flashed in alarm, ears flattened, and teeth were bared. Then, without a sound or signal, they stopped. They stopped moving altogether, like the participants of some kind of party game. Beth saw them standing there, stiff and exquisite, with only their nostrils moving, and knew that she had done this thing—this impossible thing—with her mind.

Breakfast was at eight. Angel came limping out of the house with the tray in her hands. It held a stack of white toast and a mound of eggs, which quivered when she set it down on the picnic table. There was a pitcher of ice tea, made from powder, and half a sheet of a paper towel to use as a napkin. When the weather was nice, Beth ate in the backyard. This was mostly to escape the heat and oppression of Angel's kitchen, which besides being overcrowded was decorated with a menacing wall of cast-iron trivets. Angel sat down at the picnic table and piled her dish with cold eggs. She always carried a large checkered thermos of sweet tea, which she shook while she spoke, knocking the ice around. She limped badly and was due for a knee replacement, she said. During the day, she drove her truck to garage sales, junk shops, and auctions, looking for old bridles and saddles, or mismatched pieces of driving equipment that none of the horses were trained to use. By the time she got home, Beth was in the barn, watering the horses, and she'd hear that scraping limp come up the aisle.

"I got a new one here," Angel liked to shout over the running hose. "This one only needs a few repairs." Then she would hold up an armful of leather and rusted buckles for Beth's perusal. The problem was that neither of them knew how to fix any of it, so it all ended up in a dusty trunk behind the hay.

"You've got a group of five coming at ten," Angel said through her eggs. "Don't use Penny. Her cough is worse today. King's lame, but he can take a child. But not a fat child." She shook her tea.

When Beth took the job as a trail guide, she knew almost nothing about horses. Her feet were trampled daily, her toes always purple and fat inside her narrow black boots. She had her arms bitten, leaving red ovals across her skin. And more often than not, she found herself pinned against a wall by a willfully ignorant be-hind. All of this went unnoticed by her boss, who sang her praises to the customers. "You'll be in good hands with this one," she'd say. "A real natural." Then she'd limp back into the farmhouse.

Beth gradually began to learn how to control the horses. In a cluttered upstairs room in the house, she'd found a book called *How Your Horse Wants You to Ride* and she had smuggled it back to her cabin, hidden it under her bunk. She had taken it out every night to study the diagrams, the dotted figure eights, the pear-shaped aerial view of the horse's back. None of it made any sense to her. It was like reading about how to climb the face of a cliff and then being expected to do it without falling to your death. Beth fell a lot. The horses spooked easily, often sending her sliding off the saddle, into shallow ditches or patches of brambles. Once she landed on her feet, only to discover that she'd somehow threaded a maple sapling through her T-shirt, up through the bottom and out through her armhole. Then, after getting her foot caught in the stirrup and bouncing her head against a tree stump, she had stopped riding with a saddle. This earned her more respect from the tourists, who saw this as evidence of tremendous skill. She led them up the mountain trail, twisting around on her horse's back to see behind her, and shouting at them to keep their shoulders back, to lean forward when climbing a hill. Great, that's great! she shouted to them, whether they'd done it or not. The tourists looked blandly ahead, gripping their saddle horns. Sometimes they dropped their reins altogether to flip open a cell phone, or to take a photograph. They have no idea, thought Beth. All it would take was a clap of thunder, a bee sting, a turkey vulture to land in their path and these horses would be gone, galloping back down the mountain. They were practically feral. The evidence was marked up and down her arms; she felt it cold in her stomach every time her horse stumbled over a rock or danced sideways at a gust of wind.

"Dumb old herd mentality," Angel had once admitted to her. "It's the only thing keeping them from going rogue."

The family of five walked into the barn, children first, as if they were being prodded from behind. The mother was a slim woman with a pair of sunglasses on top of her head. She looked exhausted but had a resolute expression, as if to say, *I said we'd come and here we are.* The father was a large man wearing a T-shirt that was wet in the front in a strange pattern, like he had dried his hands on it. The three boys wore baseball caps, all the brims pointed to the floor. Beth greeted them and gave the mother the release form to sign.

The family had not brought their own helmets, so they had to be fitted with extras from the big trunk in the tack room. Trouble surfaced when the two older boys realized that one of them would have to wear a girl's pink bicycle helmet. They fought over the remaining helmet until the father ambled over like he was going to box someone on the ears and jammed it onto the older boy's head. The middle boy whined and swung his arms and was further humiliated when, in addition to the girly helmet, he was made to ride a small white pony named Princess.

They rode up the trail in single file, Beth heading the line on a dark bay thoroughbred. It was ten o'clock and the day was already hot. The sun made wet ripples of light on the darker horses' hides. Tall weeds, hissing with insects, brushed the riders' toes. Beth held her reins tightly and felt her hips loosen with the broad movements of her horse as it climbed. She had put the youngest boy behind her so that she could keep an eye on him. Every time she looked back, he was staring ahead. His eyes were dark and wide and afraid.

"That's good," she encouraged him, but she believed that he was right to be scared. Deer sometimes jumped across the path and frightened the horses. Jets flew too low, plowing open the sky. They entered the forest and the trail straightened. Beth turned again to look at the line of horses behind her. The father had his feet hanging out of the stirrups, and one of his shoulders hung as if it were injured. The two older boys rode side by side, their ponies jerking their heads around to get a nip at each other. The mother rode behind them all, erect and unemotional, as if she were taking the experience very seriously and nothing had better ruin it.

Beth took them on a detour through the neighbor's cornfield. Coming out of the tree line, Beth could feel the heat, like two sharp points, boring into her bare shoulders. In the corn, it was even hotter, as the stalks blocked any hint of a breeze. The boys began to shriek.

"Corn!" they cried. "There's corn stuck on that plant! Dad, look."

"Where did you think corn came from?" the mother asked. Her horse dropped its head, blowing air. The boys continued to shout. They leaned sideways in their saddles, lunging at the stalks. Beth placed her hand on her horse's rump and twisted around, about to raise her voice, to tell the boys that this was not a carnival ride. It had begun to annoy her, lately, how people were inclined to feel so invincible, especially when thrown into a setting that they knew nothing about. But it was only the two older boys that were causing the fuss. The youngest boy, she saw now, was clutching his saddle horn, weeping into his pony's mane.

The day before, Beth had had only one customer. A man showed up during Beth's lunch break and asked to go up the mountain. He was middle-aged and white with sunscreen. Over his shirt, he wore an orange reflective vest, which he said was to alert the hunters, although it was not the season.

They had ridden in silence. At the top of the mountain, the man pulled out a disposable camera and pointed it at the view. He rolled the film and then hesitated.

"It's no use taking pictures of views," he said. He shook his head and then opened his eyes wide, like the thought had just come to him.

"You wouldn't mind standing there on your horse, would you? A picture's not worth anything without somebody in it."

Beth had urged her horse toward the edge of the cliff. She could see State Line Road from up there, the glints of passing cars. "You can see three states from up here," she said under her breath. "Vermont, New York, and Massachusetts." The tourists always laughed when she said this, expecting there to be a joke hidden in there somewhere. But it was true: you really could see three states from up there.

The man dropped his reins and snapped two pictures in a row. Then he tucked the camera back under his vest and snatched up his reins, as if he were in danger of losing control of the horse. He shrugged, and they made their way back down.

"Lean back in your saddle," Beth had said when his horse stumbled. "That's great," she said. "You're doing great." When they were back at the hitching post, the man handed her a twenty-dollar bill for a tip.

The family of five did not tip. At the end of the ride, Beth helped them down from their horses at the hitching post and gave the youngest boy a sugar cube. He had calmed down since the incident in the cornfield, but it had taken some time before anyone could understand him.

"Farmer! Farmer!" he had cried before putting his hands over his ears and slumping forward in his saddle. It seemed that he was terrified that they would encounter a farmer on their ride, as if farmers lived in the center of cornfields, like a Minotaur in a labyrinth. Beth had tried to comfort him.

"Farmers like to be in the shade this time of day. Out of the sun," she said, taking hold of the boy's reins so his pony would walk beside her horse. But the boy only shrieked louder.

"You mean, 'In the *dell*?'" he cried. Beth had caught the mother's eye from the back of the line. The woman shook her head severely, as if the boy's crisis was a commonly occurring and much-loathed family drama.

Once the family was gone, Beth untacked the horses and aimed the hose at their backs, where the saddles had made them sweat. She concentrated on the stream of water, watching it waver beneath her thumb, while the horses twitched their bellies against the droplets rolling down their sides. Beth set the hose down on the dirt and began to untie them. Once they were all free, there was a moment of quiet. The horses stood in front of the barn, water and dirt swirling around their hooves, as if they did not know what to do. Then, with uncanny precision, each animal faced the barn and walked inside. Beth watched them turn at right angles into their stalls, leaving behind the empty, freshly swept aisle. Again, she was not surprised. She had done this. She had willed it to happen. The water continued to run from the hose, creating a puddle at her feet, and she felt the goose bumps spread across her back, like liquid.

The man returned that afternoon. Again he was wearing white sunscreen and an orange reflective vest. Below were long cargo shorts and a pair of tall rain boots, which nearly reached the bottom of the shorts, leaving only his red kneecaps exposed. He had not called ahead of time to make an appointment.

"Hi," he said, when he reached the barn. Beth wondered if he had come to complain about something and wished that Angel was there and not driving around to flea markets. Her pile of dusty saddles had grown past the rim of the big trunk and was spilling over the edge. The leather was stiff and cracked, with the flaps bent upward. Neither of them knew how to soften them. The man stood in front of her, clasping his hands, his eyes set back in restful self-assuredness. It seemed that he was expecting her to do something. He was so content to stand there without speaking that Beth suddenly feared that he was there about something else entirely. Maybe he knew about what had happened with the horses. He had taken her picture, she remembered. Maybe there had been something revealed in the photograph that could not be seen with the naked eye. An aura. Some kind of misty apparition. The man reached beneath the orange vest into a pocket in his shirt and brought out a checkbook.

"Forty for an hour?" he asked her.

Beth led them up the path on her dark mare. The sun was high and white, the heat descending every time the wind let up. They passed some old apple trees, holding small, stony pieces of fruit. They passed a gray shed beaten flat on one side. Somewhere, beyond a far tree line, there was the sound of a tractor, fading in and out as it rounded the field. The man was silent, but Beth could hear his horse's careful steps. Big Red's hooves were almost as large as dinner plates, and they made a sound like crushed porcelain every time they landed on the rocky path. She twisted around and saw that the man was looking up at the sky, dreamily, with his hands brought together at his belly.

"Lean forward when you go up the hills," Beth told him.

She watched him try to stand in his stirrups and then fall heavily back into the saddle. He looked at her helplessly.

"Think about using your center of gravity to balance the horse's," she explained. The man brightened at this and lifted himself, once again incorrectly, but with more confidence.

"Perfect," she said. She remembered the terrified boy from earlier. She had a feeling that no one in that family was going to address this apparent phobia of his, that he would carry his fear of farmers silently and with shame, until it was buried by adolescence. Beth felt as though she understood the reasoning behind it, how quickly a figure as simple and seemingly harmless as a farmer could turn sinister with the right dose of imagination. She wished that she had said something more to the boy after the ride, as he had stood in front of her, chewing his sugar cube. Only she did not know what. It was not part of her job.

The lookout at the top of the mountain was a small

grassy clearing by a ledge where the tree branches bent low, creating a hole in the forest from which the riders could peer out at the sky. Beth and the man loosened their reins, letting the horses drop their heads. For a moment, there was only the sound of the horses' teeth tearing at the grass. Beth watched the white body of a hawk drifting upward. The gaps of light between the leaves swam around, blinding and watery. Beth could hear the man beside her creaking in his saddle as he adjusted his position. She turned. He was sitting with his arms at his side, staring at her with muddy, cold-blooded eyes.

When she saw it, she first imagined that it was the result of some embarrassing accident. Perhaps it had been jostled loose from all the riding, she thought. Or maybe the man had released it to relieve some kind of discomfort created by the saddle. There was something lifeless and extraneous about it, like a battered finger. It should not have been so dreadful, lying there, lamely, against the tough leather of the saddle, and yet Beth felt something inside her constrict, drawn in against danger. She could not look the man in the eye. To see his face, she thought, would be to know his intentions.

"There's been a mistake," she said, her eyes turning

to the ground. Her voice was thin. She was ashamed of the sound it made and then was overcome with shame, for the whole, ridiculous situation. There they were, she thought, on horses! Horses! She felt her mare's step beneath her, as if it were her own, as if she had sprouted long, stupid legs and didn't know how to use them. She was too high off the ground. The world around her, with its waving branches and blinking rifts of light, was unstable, riotous. Had they not been on horses, she thought, she would have done something more. Something assertive. But it was as though they were communicating through puppets, or trying to have an argument on stilts. Trembling, she turned her mare on its haunches and started back down the mountain.

"Lean back in your saddle as you ride down the hill," she called back to him. She knew that the man's horse would know what to do. It was a good, sound-minded horse, who'd once been tangled in a fence ribbon, and acted bravely, she thought. And she was thankful for it all the way down.

Your Next Breath

◆

Kitty heard that the woman's body had been found "in a state of decomposition." She knew that this meant that it was awful—too awful to describe to the public. It would have seemed sadistic to do so, in even the coldest, most clinical terms, like explaining to a small child the manner in which their dog had died. She knew that it must have been the kind of sight that her father would have seen during his years as a detective, the kind of atrocity that he must have carried home with him, she imagined, stuck to the inside of his head, like the smoke damage on the ceiling above their stove. Her father was always promising to have the ceiling fixed, or to have it "looked at," which sounded hopeful and vague enough for Kitty's mother, who was probably too tired to care much about it, as long as it was out of her hands. "It's being looked at," was a phrase that people could live on for a long time.

There were so many ways of being delicate with reality. "A state of decomposition" did not really tell you anything, but you felt comforted in knowing that you had been told all that you ought to have been told. You were given a sense that someone else—some other person of qualified constitution—was handling the psychological aftermath. The truth was that there was no such person.

Growing up, Kitty had overheard all sorts of details about crimes or horrific accidents that had happened in town. There were many nights that she had risen innocently from her bed to use the toilet, only to become transfixed outside her parents' bedroom, her father speaking to her mother about things that had not made it into the news articles. When Kitty was in the tenth grade, a girl in the grade above her went missing over the Christmas break. It was very cold—even for Vermont that time of year—and a search had begun at the lake, which was frozen over. Volunteers had gathered to break the ice, to look under the water, volunteers who must have eventually hoped to find the girl—even if it meant confirming the worst—just so they could go home and eat a warm meal. And those who might have been hoping this got their wish. The girl's body was discovered wedged under the ice where the lake narrowed and the current picked up. This was what the people at Kitty's school knew, although the announcement of the death did not mention the cause or circumstances. This was what the volunteers knew, those who had come close to the body and those who had found only snow and more snow. Kitty, however, who should not have known anything, had heard her father talking about a diary that was found in a pillowcase, tucked under the girl's bed, in which the girl had expressed her wish to die. "THEY WILL ACCEPT ME, OR I WILL DROWN." An ultimatum, probably never spoken aloud, and found only when it was much too late. But, Kitty had wondered, had the girl, in writing these bold words, really known what she was committing herself to? Was the pain of being misunderstood by her peers, or her family—whoever "they" were—worse than the panic of being sucked into the dark water, of throwing out your hands and meeting the slick underside of a layer of ice? Was it worse than the realization—that slow chill of perfect comprehension—that there was no one around to line up your next breath?

Kitty experienced an echo of this feeling years later, when she heard about what Danny had done to that poor woman. This was not just a rumor, or a terrible misunderstanding. Danny had, in fact, taken a life and he had done so intentionally, followed by a full confession. Kitty had first thought of Danny's hands, the countless times that they had reached for her, the ease with which they found her in the mornings, like the flowing of water downhill, or a puppy stumbling blindly to its mother. He had always been warm, stripping his clothes before bed, while she shivered and closed the window that he had cracked when she was not in the room to protest. She tried to attach something predictive to his unnatural warmth of body. "Cold hands; warm heart," she had heard people say. Could the opposite apply? When she remembered how she had once craved the heat of his skin, her body bristled—even in the wake of his crimes—her breasts, which had always felt the cold most acutely, piqued with a faint stirring of longing. She told herself that it was a very faint stirring. It was only a physical inclination, which would always lag behind the mind in integrity.

There had been a dog, a stout, medium-sized dog with a stump for a tail that wiggled happily, although the tail had seemed to Kitty like something that should not have the power of animation. The dog belonged to Danny's landlady but had access to the entire apartment complex and preferred to spend the nights with Danny, who allowed her to lick his dirty dishes, even the steak knives, which had made Kitty nervous. Besides the tail stump, there were other things about the dog that had irritated Kitty during that time, mainly that her name was Mama, but also that Danny insisted on showering her with affection and expensive dog food.

"You already pay rent," Kitty had liked to remind him. "You shouldn't have to feed the woman's dog as well. Have you called about the leak above the shower yet?" Kitty often felt that Danny was a bit naïve, or, at worst, that he was using naïveté as a disguise for laziness.

"Oh, Mama," he would croon, and the dog would lay her fat head in his palm while the stump twitched obscenely.

Kitty felt that the town's response to the news was eerily understated. People were, of course, shocked. Old high school friends of Danny's seemed to find comfort in the notion that the Danny that they had known—the *old*

Danny—would be the one to occupy their memories. They believed that they could break their love for him in two, discarding the half that was spoiled. One man had made a statement on his online profile: "I don't care what he did. Danny will always be the boy with dimples who could not ride a bicycle." There were people doing their part to preserve versions of Danny that were inarguably lovable, but no one was showing up to challenge his guilt. The notion that Danny was still existing and sitting stagnant in a prison cell did not seem to register with anyone whom Kitty talked to.

The woman's name was Angelica Place. When Kitty saw the pictures of her on the news, she thought—and could not help but think—That woman is too much for Danny, which did not really mean anything, except that Kitty had always pictured Danny dating a certain, docile type of woman. Angelica was broad in her features, with shoulder-length black hair and a petulant, downward turn to her mouth that somehow indicated humor and intensity and worlds of strength. The news said that she had been an accomplished English show jumper, on track to the Olympics. They stressed this point, as if to say that denying this woman her glory was crueler than denying her her life. There were also images of her horse, a charcoal-colored gelding with a distinguished sloping face—a Trakehner, the caption read, which Kitty had to look up and found to be a breed originating in Prussia, known for its aptitude in dressage. Kitty found herself preoccupied with these details—Angelica's potential, her handsome face, the handsomeness and good breeding of her horse. The news stories were a source of outpouring for this woman's merits, as if the world were insatiable for proof that she did not deserve to die.

Kitty and Danny had cut contact a decade ago out of respect for Kitty's husband—now ex-husband—Drew. Drew had not liked Danny, and it was not just because he and Kitty had dated.

"I believe the man to be a sociopath," Drew had said of Danny, and it was much easier for Kitty to agree than to be caught defending a man for whom she was no longer supposed to have any emotional investment. What Kitty had never dared voice to her husband, or to anyone else, was that Danny had said the same of Drew, when Kitty first began dating Drew.

"Oh, Kitty," he had said to her, for they used to keep in touch, now and again meeting for coffee. Danny stirred crystals of raw sugar into his latte and licked the spoon. "I've known Drew since elementary school. I'm pretty sure that he's a sociopath." Danny's reasoning stemmed from a sixth-grade trip to a veterinarian's office, where eleven-year-old Drew had opened a can marked BIOHAZ-ARD and tried to touch a pile of surgical waste.

The girl who had thrown herself into the icy lake used to be in Kitty's homeroom. Kitty remembers now that they had known each other, very briefly, in this way. The girl, whose name had started with an *M*—McKenzie? Madeline?—would slump over her desk and inspect the strands of her long, honey-colored hair until she found one that was split at the end. Then she would, with great concentration, snip the affected strand with her shiny, acrylic fingernails. This behavior might have been in-terpreted as sullenness, but Kitty supposed that it was no different than her own inclination to fill in the typed letter *O*s in her science textbook with a ballpoint pen. She was not supposed to do this, but she sometimes felt that she could not relax, that she could not breathe as deeply, if she did not just fill in the *O*s—and possibly the lowercase *b*'s and *p*'s.

After M's death, a lecturer was called in to speak to grades nine through twelve about the dangers of bullying. The students were encouraged to break up their cliques, to smother their solitary, unpopular peers with acceptance and friendship. If it was discovered that even one person was sitting alone in the cafeteria at lunchtime, then it would be considered the failure of the entire student body. This came as terrible news to Kitty and others like her, who looked forward to their lunch break so that they could put on headphones and daydream. What had been her one solace became representative of an overall failure to be kind.

In truth, M had not been a victim of bullying. She had seemed to fall comfortably into the middle range of most categories, of beauty and intelligence and athleticism. She was perfectly passable, which, in high school, could have been considered a blessing. Her father, a short-statured and likable man, ran a small landscaping business in town and her mother volunteered three times a year to hand-make every costume needed for the school plays. It was a tremendous feat that no one could turn down. It would take ten volunteers to replace her. When she insisted on continuing this tradition after her daughter's death, the theater director was cornered into a deep and humble acceptance. Black-and-white play-bills were printed in M's memory.

Kitty could not remember anyone having anything cruel to say about M, or any instance of someone treating her unfairly. No one that Kitty had talked to could remember such a thing.

"She was just *there*," one boy from her gym class said. "And now she's not." Perhaps it was exactly this kind of existence that M had decided to rid herself of.

After he and Kitty lost touch, Danny purchased a small house on some wooded property that had no potential to be anything other than a ditch-ridden, barely traversable maze of sticks. Angelica's body had been found someplace in the midst of this, buried under a heap of large stones.

"To keep the coyotes away is my guess," said Kitty's father, who had since retired but was kept well informed of the town's criminal activity. His theory was weakened, however, by the fact that whoever had arranged the rocks had spared the woman's face, leaving it exposed to the elements. Kitty did not want to suggest that Danny had intended this part of her to be the scavengers' first target, or that, alternately, he had returned to the scene afterward and moved the stones away, to get one last look. Both scenarios could, in Kitty's reasoning, be taken as a sign of sentimentality. She had known Danny to be sentimental.

Kitty remembered the careful way in which Danny had wrapped Christmas presents and how dumbfounded he had been when he discovered that she did not know how.

"What do you mean you don't know how to wrap a present? Are you just sloppy at taping the corners?"

No, she had answered, a little embarrassed, but tipsy and amused with herself at the same time.

"I actually don't understand what to do at all. How does it not end up a giant crumpled ball every time?"

Danny had looked at her as though his world was about to collapse. She had rubbed his back.

"Poor baby," she laughed. "You're dating a monster."

And then there was the day that the landlady's dog died. It was only sudden in the sense that Danny had been unaware that the dog—his beloved Mama—was so old. It was not until three days after the death that the landlady thought to inform her tenants. Danny sulked but had not grieved openly. In place of tears, he seemed to suffer a malfunction in muscle memory. He continued to hold the door open when he got home from work, expecting the dog to follow him through. And he could not stop putting his plate on the floor beside his chair after he had finished eating. Sometimes he waited a full minute for the dog to trot into the kitchen at the sound, before he realized his mistake.

A week after Mama died, Danny did it again. He pushed his scraps into a little pile at the edge of his plate—the last crescent of a cheeseburger and a few cold cooked carrots—and lowered the dish to the floor. Kitty, who was also sitting at the table, watched him. She watched his hand return to his lap, his conversation focused on her, while the old expectation ticked in the back of his head, like a wind-up toy that still surges forward when you nudge it. She saw the instant that the expectation died and was replaced by awareness. Danny's hand moved slowly back down, feeling for the plate without lowering his eyes, as if he could keep Kitty from noticing, if only their eyes remained locked. He would not want to be faced with her amusement and pity, her lips sealed in generosity.

"What?" He was standing now. His eyes were bright, darting over her face in a series of small, sharp assessments. He hooked his arm around her neck, pulling her head uncomfortably toward his chest. "You gonna make fun of me? Go ahead."

They moved across the kitchen in a strange, upright wrestling match, each person trying to overpower the other, without any clearly defined objective. Kitty remembers how Danny looked at her, narrow and intent and full of laughter, as he pushed her toward the wall. She thought: He is going to push me up against the wall and kiss me, like in a movie.

And he almost did this—it seemed as though that was where they were headed, had he not been distracted by the open broom closet. Kitty watched him measure the closet in one swift glance, as if that was how the decision to shove her in there was made—based on whether or not she would fit. He used his hands to pin her arms against her side, and the force of his chest, leaning in, to throw her off-balance. She allowed it—she must have allowed it, she decided afterward—out of playfulness or curiosity, or that same compliance that she sometimes adopted when she wanted to call his bluff. He closed the door on her and she knocked her fists against the inside and called him an asshole. She was laughing, still caught up in the exhilaration of the moment, her heart drumming deep in her ears, until she heard the scrape of the lock slide into place. It was not a primal panic that set in, meaning that Kitty did not fear for her life directly. Somewhere in her mind there was still the knowledge that it was only a broom closet, that this was only a prank; Danny could not possibly have the cruelty and the endurance to keep her trapped in there for as long as it would take for her to asphyxiate, or starve. And somehow, she felt that her fear was darker than that, that it was born from a place inside, near the base of her spine, like an explosion of hormones, or a seed bursting from a pod. In a way, she was giving birth to this feeling and many more like it. *I am a vessel*, it said. *And I have been letting the world pass through me—water, food, air, and even men—and I have not thought to question it until now.*

"Hey," she called to him. "Hey! I don't go in here!" As if she were an irate butter knife placed in the wrong drawer. The closet swung open and there was Danny, grinning at her, his face shining with sweat.

"I don't *go* in here?" he echoed her, as if what she had said was immensely cute. "I don't *go* in here? *That's* what you have to say?" His hands slid up her waist, his mouth on her neck, nibbling her behind her ears.

It seemed that his arousal had peaked at this one sentence of hers.

"You're adorable," he said, pulling away again to look at her and taking a lock of her hair that had, in all the chaos, fallen in front of her eyes. He tucked it behind her ear, smoothing it carefully back into place, and she could feel the warmth of his hand, radiant against her cheek, as if he had been holding it over a fire.

Gorgon

◆

When I was ten years old, there was a boy in my class named Richie Ross, who was well respected among the older children because he had a pet iguana that would cling to his head when he rode his bicycle. He was the kind of kid who found it humorous to pretend to be a dog all day. He might sit at his desk with his tongue hanging out, or answer the teacher's question with a bark. Often, he would try to confuse the substitute teacher, convincing her that we were allowed to go to the bathroom in twos, or that we always took a nap after lunch—things that no one actually wanted to do, things we were less impressed by than annoyed by. I was able to ignore him for the most part, until he began to harass me on the playground. I had been playing by the fence, where an old tree trunk had grown into the wire, the bark bulging through the chain-link, like bread rising. Richie came over. He was making a strange motion with his hands, wringing them together while squealing from the corner of his mouth. He asked me if I wanted to have sex, if I thought about it, and if I washed my vagina. At the time, I thought of it as a kind of trick question, the truthful answer being: no, no, and yes, but that's none of your business. But, not wanting to give the impression that I was cooperating at all, I just said, "No," and I walked away.

The next day, someone wrote "JENNY CLARKE HAS A DIRTY PUSSY" on the chalkboard when the class was out for lunch. It was immediately wiped away, but as with most chalkboards, the message's ghost could not be erased fully without a wet sponge and so it remained on our minds throughout the afternoon. I probably found this less upsetting than the teacher, because at the time, while I understood its implications, I assumed that *pussy* was an arbitrary euphemism, made up by Richie on the spot. Somehow this belief made it more a problem of his than it was of mine.

◆

Earlier that summer, my parents had taken me on a whale watch in Cape Cod. Excited, I had outfitted myself with a pair of binoculars, a purple baseball cap, and a "Save the Whales" pin on my chest. I had studied whales in school and had made a very nice blue whale from papier-mâché, which the teacher hung from the ceiling and kept there even as I moved up a grade. I had expectations about whales. On the whale watch I kept my eyes on the water, concentrating on the broken ribbons of light, the many small waves that looked misleadingly like dorsal fins. We saw a blast of mist and suddenly they were all around us with their battered gray backs, their blowholes that closed tightly, like lips. I ran up and down the deck of the boat, trying to see them as best as I could. I pushed past other children and stuck my head through the guardrails. But what I found disappointed me. The whales seemed much too small. They were no longer than the boat, no wider than a car. I wanted the whales to be colossal, terrifying. I wanted eyes as wide as my kitchen table, teeth the size of mailboxes.

At the time, I liked monsters. I liked tales of the impossible. Myths and legends. When I was very young, my father set up a cassette player on the table by my bed, so I could listen to stories as I fell asleep. My favorites were the Greek myths, where everyone was moody and restless and supernaturally beautiful, unless they were monstrous. I especially liked the story of Medusa, a snake-haired creature, who was so ugly that the sight of her turned people to stone. I was fascinated and horrified by this concept and would often have nightmares in which some terrible thing lay around a corner and it was inevitable that I must pass it. If I could get by without looking, I would be fine, but my eyelids would become faulty and when I threw up my hands to shield my face, I saw that they were made of glass, or flimsy, like paper. The idea that sight might be linked to death was unbearable for me. Still, I listened to that story every night—how Perseus was able to gaze upon her unharmed by using a mirror, how he beheaded her and then kept the severed head, to be used as a weapon against his enemies. I sometimes wondered if this head still existed, if it and its powers were immortal. It might show up anywhere, it occurred to me, and whoever was unlucky enough to find it would be defenseless. They wouldn't have a chance. It became habit for me to close the shower curtain before I used the bathroom, to shield my eyes when I opened the refrigerator, or the kitchen cabinets. The head, I reasoned, would be less of a threat to me if I was always expecting it. There was a toolshed outside with a round slice of glass missing from one of the windows that I avoided at all costs, for fear of what bodiless thing might be waiting there to be seen.

The head showed up on the day that Richie Ross wrote that awful message about me on the chalkboard. School had adjourned and I had walked home as usual. I remember that it was raining and some of the boys from my class were gathered along the edge of the sidewalk, waving to the cars, hoping that one of them would swerve and create a large wave of water. Because of this, I did not take my usual route. Instead, I cut through the driveway of a large tenement building to where I knew there to be a path through the woods. This path eventually passed by my backyard, although the trees were so thick that I sometimes misjudged and ended up at the neighbor's instead. The woods were a common place for teenagers to hang out, and I knew that at least one of them hid a stash of magazines in the cleavage of an old tree. That day the underbrush was heavy with rain and the ground was peaty and the wet soil rose up the spines of the ferns. The birds' voices were garbled and nectary and I could feel the humidity curling my hair. I climbed the stone wall, glistening with slug trails, at the end of my property and saw my house sitting there shaded by pines. There was something drowsy, or drugged about its appearance, the pine boughs weighted by rain, the gutters dripping, and the dark windows. I was uneasy, approaching it from behind like that, as if I were sneaking up on some dozing beast. I felt very strange, almost compelled to knock at the door instead of letting myself in, and when I did go inside, the house was cold and unwelcoming. I found my father in the kitchen, prepping for dinner. He had taken off his tie but remained in his shirt, with the sleeves rolled up to his elbows. I sat at the table and watched him work, listening to the cork-popping sound of chopped carrots, the small hiss of onions under the knife. Hunched over the counter, he was so tall that all he had to do to reach a high cupboard was to straighten slightly. I realized that every time he opened a drawer, or a cupboard, or stooped to check the oven, I was holding my breath, as if I expected to see something ghastly hidden there. Somehow, it all came together for me in that moment: that my father had given me the story tapes—perhaps unconsciously, as if by fate—so that I would hear the Medusa story and know what to do. The notion that it was her head, now that she had been killed, that was the threat made it all the more believable and terrifying. Its existence was theoretical, chaotic, like a disease, or a natural disaster.

I began to search my bedroom—my closet, my dresser, the space beneath my bed. I threw books from the shelf, I disemboweled my nesting dolls, all the while holding my hand over my eyes. I ransacked the place until the commotion caused my father to come upstairs. His hands were large and warm around my face and smelled like onions. He was bewildered. My room was in total disarray, the clothes spilling out of my drawers, the lampshade detached, lightbulb bare and hot. Why had I done this? I had no answer for him and finally, having left the stove on, my father was forced to return to the kitchen. Only then did I realize that there was one place that I had missed. In my closet there was a false ceiling that could be reached by climbing the low metal bar that ran across the closet's width. I tended to avoid opening it, because the crawl space that it led to was dark and, I imagined, full of cobwebs. This time, however, I closed my eyes as I pushed against the ceiling and reached my hand in, sliding my palm along walls, inching it forward until I felt the head there, slippery and cold, like a dead octopus. With my eyes still closed I climbed down, found the window, and thrust it outside. I heard the heavy crash as it fell through the first then second layer of brush below.

The next morning I said goodbye to my father and began to walk to school. My street ran alongside the woods, the heavy maple leaves hanging low over the sidewalk so that they dripped water down your back if you brushed them. The sidewalk remained the same height while the ground sloped downward so that if you jumped off the edge through the guardrail you would find yourself eye level with the road. I walked to the stop sign and looked behind me. Our house was barely visible through the trees, its white paint like flecks of eggshell behind the branches. I ducked under the top bar of the guardrail, bracing myself against a sapling that showered me with hard, tepid drops, and lowered myself to the ground. From there, I could just see the shining tires of the passing cars. I waited there, hearing the cars approach and then slow, creaking slightly, to a stop at the intersection. I waited, water itching the back of my neck, until I saw my father's car roll quietly down the road. It stopped, something within it shifted and settled, and then something within it picked itself back up and the car continued through the stop sign.

Skipping school felt dangerous to me, not for the anticipated consequences, but for that window of time when I imagined the teacher would wait for me to appear in class, that horrible moment when someone might say, "Where's Jenny?" and I wouldn't be there to defend myself. I was about to pull myself back up to the sidewalk when I heard a pattering sound. I turned around and saw a man, about ten feet away, facing the trunk of a tree. Between him and the tree, at the man's feet, there was a stack of yellow phone books, the pages dark gray and rippled. Some small thing seemed to be hopping on them and then I saw that it was a stream of liquid, hitting the sodden yellow covers. The man was urinating. He zipped up and turned, standing in front of the phone books, as if trying to hide them. His beard was white below his bottom lip and dark blond at the bottom, like it had been dipped in oil. He looked at me with an annoyed but relieved look, then put out his hands, walking slowly toward me. I should have climbed back onto the sidewalk then, but I believed that, having caught him in such a vulnerable act, I owed him some chance to recover himself. He came very close to me, so close that I could smell his clothing. It smelled like some burned thing that had been stuffed into a hole and then unearthed.

"Ah," he said. "Here she is." There was something ironic in his voice, some low, suffering drawback, that made me wonder if I was supposed to know him, if I was offending him by not. His hand came forward and picked something off my temple. It was a very small slug, the kind that might attach itself to a leaf and rain down upon you with the rest of the seeds and bits of flower debris. I watched the man roll the slug between his forefinger and thumb before dropping it to the ground.

My best friend Alicia used to dream that an invisible man would come into her room at night and lift her from her bed. The invisible man would carry her around town, showing her the darkened shop windows, the blinking intersections, and the sleeping dogs. He would hold her out slightly whenever there was something that he wanted her to see, like someone offering a baby to be held. And then he would carry her back home, tuck her into her bed, and kiss her goodnight. Years passed and she either stopped having the dream or she stopped telling me about it. In sixth grade, she transferred to a private school, and by the time we were in high school and she had transferred back into the public school system, we no longer knew how to speak to each other. I eventually stopped waving to her in the hallways, because it felt childish. I think we were both relieved.

I must admit that I was jealous of Alicia's invisible man. There was something exhilarating about the idea of being stolen from your bed, to be conveyed silently through the night. I sometimes dreamed of men, achingly—never one specific man, just the lone presence of one, like a baritone heat wave in the dark. I usually woke from these dreams strangely grieved, imagining that I wanted something that did not exist in the world, as if no one in the history of humankind had ever wanted a man like I did. As if they did not exist in the capacity that I longed for them. It seemed to me that Alicia's invisible man was one step ahead of the aching, masculine presence in my dream, if not fully developed, then at least solid, responsive. And it seemed to go hand in hand that Alicia would mature faster, would be noticed sooner. Her body began to embarrass me, as if all that we had ever whispered in secrecy was rising to the surface. Her eyes grew sleek with sexual knowledge. She reminded me of a young pregnant cat—a tiny, insecure thing of great importance.

After meeting the man in the woods, I climbed back onto the sidewalk and walked home. I had a powerful inclination that the head had returned, that it was lurking in some unexpected corner, waiting to turn the first person to find it into stone. Normally, it was my father who arrived at the house before me and there was no way to warn him, to explain to him the danger there. So I went inside with my eyes closed and my hands outstretched. I found it easily, in the vegetable drawer beside a large cabbage. I could have thrust the head in front of the mirror and gazed upon the reflection like Perseus had done— the lacquered hills of the face, glaring back at me, like something pulled from a bog. But I didn't risk it.

The story of Medusa, as it was recorded on my *Myths and Legends* cassette tape, ended with the birth of Pegasus. Pegasus, a white, winged stallion, was said to have sprung from the pool of blood issued from the hole in Medusa's neck. He was fully grown, completely un-stained, and he flew up to the heavens, where he re-mained, delivering lightning and thunder to Zeus. I did not like this ending. I did not like the cool and arrogant way in which the narrator, a British woman, described it, like a cheery nurse explaining a very painful proce-dure. There seemed to be an underlying smugness to the whole thing, as if the storyteller herself were conspiring against me. *Isn't it just the way it is,* she seemed to say, *that innocence would be born of evil?* It felt like a lesson that I did not want to learn, like being told by an adult to give up a fear that you are holding on to very tightly. Accepting this would mean being flung headlong into a kind of nihilistic maturity, where everyone turns up dead in the end, but the audience applauds anyway. I sometimes wonder: If there had been a touch of irony, just a drop of regret in her voice, would I have turned out differently? Would I have been altered, reformed—tamed, like a monster shown a kindness?

Richie continued to bother me on the playground for an-other two weeks before he dumped me for another girl.

It felt as though I had been both spared and rejected. The unfortunate girl's name was Cameron Wright. Her father had an antique car with large spoked wheels and a shrill, train-like whistle. For this reason, I had always considered her to be untouchable. The car was neither cool nor uncool. It distinguished her as "the girl with the old car." It was shocking that Richie would choose her, in the same way that it was shocking whenever someone chose the color gray.

I'd like to say that my troubles at home ended as well, that the two instances were tied neatly together, but things only became more complicated. The man from the woods had begun spending nights in the shed in the backyard. I could see him from my window, sitting on the stoop with his long legs stretched out. Sometimes he would eat a whole box of doughnuts and then smoke a cigarette. I could smell the smoke from my bedroom, like a whiff of bad breath. By mornings, he was always gone.

I did not tell my father about this for fear that there would be a confrontation. So, for many nights, I stayed awake, watching him from my window. He would come up from the woods, a tall, bowlegged silhouette with a winter cap on his head. As much as I feared him, I could not look away as long as he sat outside the shed door, cracking sunflower seeds, or picking stones from the soles of his shoes. He performed these tasks with a slow deliberateness, as if he were not trespassing but setting himself up to go fishing for an afternoon. And every now and then he would cast his gaze toward my window and I would startle, convinced that the meeting of our eyes would cause a disturbance like a firecracker, great enough to wake my father, who had been sleeping peacefully all this time, unaware of what was going on.

Prepare Her

◆

"The girl has to poop," Rachel tells the school. "Doctor's orders." This last bit is not a lie, although it feels like one, maybe because Rachel has never said "doctor's orders" in her life. There is also something questionable—rebellious even—about the idea of keeping her daughter home when she is not contagious.

"Poor thing," says the school's director. "We'll be thinking of her. We'll be sending her positive vibes."

"Yes. I will let her know," Rachel says, and, as she hangs up the phone, she decides that she will indeed tell her daughter this. She has tried every method that she can think of—prunes, warm baths, hot drinks, promises of chocolate chips and sodas. There have been scare tactics, which Rachel regrets—threats of having to go to the hospital, of complicated, invasive measures. She might as well let her daughter know that her whole pre-school is rooting for her.

Bianca won't be embarrassed, Rachel thinks. Or is it that Rachel has forgotten that shame is an opportun-ist, its means subtle and unfair? When she was Bianca's age, she watched her mother drop an egg on the kitchen floor. It landed with a slap of yellow, leaving a thin, snot-like thread across the toe of her shoe. This had filled her with humiliation, as if the thing had come from her own body, like some kind of unsightly discharge that was beyond her control. She began to cry and then to wail, and her mother did not know what to do with her.

"I don't know what to do with you," her mother said. Rachel's sorrow was unrecognizable, alien, dysfunctional.

Downstairs, Bianca is on the couch nibbling a piece of celery. The television is showing some kind of nature program. A volcano erupting. Veins of bright orange lava against a matte-black earth.

"I would just walk around the lava," Bianca says haughtily. The celery hangs from her mouth. She has not actually ingested any of it, but has only bitten the tip into a wet, stringy mess.

They have been to the doctor, who has suggested things like making "poop muffins," with bran and psyllium husk—simple, wholesome measures that Rachel is certain they are now beyond. Bianca has refused the toilet for five days. The pain comes in sharp, urgent waves and still she refuses, clenching her fists, dancing on her toes, anything to keep herself from going.

This has become a psychological struggle, Rachel realizes. The solution is somewhere in her daughter's head, which is already, at four years old, filled with strange, fiercely sophisticated ideas. On the television, a scientist in a fire-resistant suit pokes a stick into one of the lava flows and pulls it up, slowly, as if he is stretching taffy. It does look harmless. It all looks so slow and harmless.

Rachel has been living with her mother now for six months, ever since she and her husband separated. Rachel's mother is hurt and perplexed by the separation. It was entirely Rachel's fault. It was not toxic and voluminous like her mother's divorce. There is nothing impressive and darkly human and novelistic about the way her daughter's relationship deteriorated. It simply ended, without mystery or confusion. A waste.

Rachel herself is not pleased with the way things

have turned out. For one, she wishes that her mother's house were not so far from town. She feels helpless out here, buried in snow, beneath the creaking trees, the steep, forbidding face of the mountain. She keeps forgetting to buy things at the grocery store, ingredients that slip her mind during the thirty-minute drive. When she arrives back and remembers that they are still out of peanut butter, or baby carrots, or dish sponges, she feels a sort of desperation, as if she is starving. She opens bags of potato chips, thrusting her arm noisily inside while setting groceries on the shelf. She can't stop. She is starving.

Rachel writes for a magazine, which was fine while she was living off her husband's income. She felt a rush of false opulence whenever she opened a check, this marvelous piece of extra money that represented her independence, the heroism of late-night multitasking. But now she knows that the money holds little significance. She has just finished writing an article about coffee, how it does not pair well with fruit. She contacted experts on the subject, experts with headshots that were somehow both angelic and murderous. They told her that coffee did not taste good with fruit.

"Too much acid," they told her. She had written the

article despite being sick and having to care for Bianca, who was also unwell. "Most likely the flu," the doctor said. "But knowing for sure won't make a difference in how I treat you. Or how you feel."

Yes, thought Rachel. It will.

She took Bianca back home and they wrapped themselves in a blanket on the couch and when her mother returned from her job at the hospital and walked wearily across the living room, dangling her keys, Rachel called out, "We have the flu!" Because it would make a difference to her mother, whose sympathy was contingent on that sort of thing.

It is not just the separation that Rachel's mother disapproves of. When her mother is at home, she holds a constant, irritable vigilance. She opens the refrigerator and peers inside, challenging its contents, shaking the milk carton, peeling open the lid to the yogurt to check its level. She steps over toys left on the floor with great, elderly sighs. At the table, she quizzes Bianca on hypothetical moral dilemmas.

"If you had four chocolate chips, but Nana only got two, what would you do?"

"I would build a wall around my chocolate chips so you didn't see."

Rachel's mother looks at Rachel over her grand-daughter's head, a deeply troubled, warning look.

There is something that Rachel hasn't tried, something that she has been avoiding. The doctor advised letting the child do it herself. At four and a half, she has the dexterity, said the doctor. *Dexterity.* It is a clean, mechanical-sounding word that does not take into consideration her daughter's stubbornness, her skepticism, her outrageous, practically feral imagination.

On the television, the volcano is still spurting lava, thickly, and sluggishly. Bianca watches rapt, the chewed stick of celery discarded beside her on the couch cushion.

"I have something that might help," says Rachel, switching off the television. She clasps her hands together, fortifying herself against insult and objections.

But Bianca is not insulted. In fact, she is surprisingly eager to try. Rachel watches a mature and businesslike hope settle across her daughter's face as they walk, holding hands, to the upstairs bathroom. It occurs to her that Bianca has reached a degree of suffering that has made this resolve possible. She, a child who won't even try a new flavor of ice cream for fear that it won't be her favorite, will do this strange, unheard-of thing, because she wants to stop the pain. Rachel feels this reality seep into her chest like a leak, warping and blistering a wall—the damage of another small heartbreak.

In the bathroom, Rachel takes the cap off the suppository and hands it to Bianca. It is a clear plastic bulb with a long tube, or spout, at one end. The girl takes it, looks at it with cool consideration, and points the tip toward her bottom.

"Now what?" she asks.

"Well," says Rachel, "first of all, you have to move it closer."

"Like this?"

"Closer."

"Like this?"

"Even closer."

Bianca is confused.

"When do I squeeze it?" she asks.

"When it is in," Rachel says.

"In *where*?"

It is here that Rachel begins to suspect that her

daughter has been misled in some way. She recalls their brief conversation downstairs, examining it for errors or ambiguities. No, she thinks. I explained it properly. She knew what she was getting into.

"In the"—Rachel struggles for a moment. She does not want to use any terminology that might alarm the girl.

"Hole," she says. It is the best that she can do, given her options.

"What hole?"

"The one in your bottom."

A nervous, imperious fury begins to take over Bianca's features. She drops the suppository on the floor.

"I do not have a hole in my bottom."

Rachel exhales. She has been poised, encouragingly, on her knees, but now she sinks down, resting her palms against the cold tile. It is not her own, biting, self-critical voice that she hears at first, but her mother's, followed by her husband's. How could you let her reach this age without knowing? This is basic anatomy. This is vital to a proper and healthy self-image. You have failed to prepare her, they say, although Rachel has only a feeble, closed-minded understanding of what this means. Prepare her. It means more than she wants it to. She is on the verge of something terrible, something unspeakable, when she laughs.

"Okay," she says, softly. "We don't have to do this."

From the beginning, Rachel's husband has been calm and insistent about the process. He is a lawyer. He has seen how ugly divorces can be, how men and women turn to pettiness, as if picking up a new and aggressive addiction. He has always imagined (and has congratulated himself in doing so) that, in delivering these small jabs of pettiness, it is not a reward that they are after, but rather the avoidance, at all costs, of emptiness, meaninglessness, and regret. He knew of a woman who, rather than allow her husband to take the dog, had instead driven the animal—an eight-year-old shepherd—to the edge of a state forest and let it loose.

"What kind of high must you be on?" Rachel's husband had asked her. "What kind of raving, diabolical high?"

Rachel suspects that her husband has always known just how he will react under the same circumstances. She can also sense his satisfaction, the clean, uncomplicated triumph of being blameless. He has taken the blow, the shock and humiliation of it, but he will not be amazed by the aftermath.

Before the separation was imminent and they spoke to each other in only polite, distrustful language, Rachel and her husband used to argue. Rachel remembers these arguments with astonishment—how easily they fell into playful civility whenever Bianca wandered into the room and then how powerfully they worked themselves back up again when she left, like an engine, hot and ready. They would argue until there was nothing to do but reconcile, which they managed to do firmly, with concessions made on both sides. It was uncomfortable for both of them to see the other defeated. It was lonely to win an argument and so they worked just as hard to keep it fair as they did trying to strike the other down. But eventually this arrangement left Rachel bewildered. She did not have the constitution that her husband had for debate and would often carry his words with her long after they had made up, trying to make them useful, but failing, as if experimenting with strange spices. He wanted her to be more assertive, if not for her own sake, then for Bianca's. One afternoon he came home early and overheard the last minutes of one of her phone conversations. She can't remember exactly what was said.

She might have laughed, she might have said thank you more than once, let her voice rise to an unnatural servile pitch. Phone calls make her nervous. Their conditions are tight and airless, squeezing her into compliance no matter how ordinary the circumstances.

"You let people push you around," he said. "Whoever that was, you're letting them have too much power."

"It was an interview," she told him. "I'm writing a story on unoaked wine."

"*That's* how you do an interview?" He was incredulous, concerned. His anger had a focused, terrifying benevolence.

He encouraged her to have more friends, successful friends with interesting lives. It would be good for Bianca to be around strong, driven women. But Rachel could not work up the nerve. She saw these women dropping off their children at the preschool on their way to work. They looked busy. They looked tired. They had clean hair. They did not need her friendship. She thought of these women when her husband came home at the end of the day.

"What did you two do today?" he would ask, and she would think, I watched Bianca twirl in her new dress exactly fifty-eight times. I spent fifteen minutes trying to convince her to eat a bite of scrambled egg. I brushed the hair on one side of her head but did not push my luck with the other. I forgot to be spectacular.

Soon their arguments lost their vigor, their morale. Rachel had lost her stamina, and her husband seemed to be missing something, too, some roundness or element of security in his voice that used to keep Rachel from feeling afraid of him. Now she was afraid of his logic and his intellect, of the harm that they were capable of. As a kind of preparation, she began to argue with herself during the day while he was at work, muttering, prodding her opinions, searching them for weaknesses. This way, she thought, he can't get to them first.

"I know it's terrible," she'd say as she carried dinner to the table.

"I've been a lazy mother today," she would tell him as he was walking in the door.

This was not received well. "You can't say these things in front of Bianca," Rachel's husband told her. "She can't hear you putting yourself down." And Rachel felt dizzy, disarmed, the blows coming at her in all the wrong directions. Of course, she thought. *Bianca.*

◆

Bianca won't eat. It is lunchtime and she is under the kitchen table, folded in half, her arms crossed over her stomach.

"Help," she moans. "I'm *dying.*"

Amazing, Rachel thinks, how quickly sympathy gets traded for exhaustion, how easily someone else's pain becomes commonplace. She has caught herself wanting Bianca to get better for the wrong reasons—so she can go to school tomorrow, so Rachel's mother doesn't come home and find them like this. She is frustrated. She is murderous. She wishes she could take the girl's suffering upon herself, because she would know what to do with it, how to force it into submission. From here, she thinks, on her knees, rattling a box of raisins, everything looks so infuriatingly simple.

"I'm *dying!*" Bianca cries. "I'm going to faint!" She looks up at her mother with steady, reproachful intelligence. "Why did you even *have* me if I'm just going to die?"

It is too much. Rachel gets up and puts the raisins back into the cupboard. She wants to call her husband to tell him what their daughter has just said. She feels momentarily and sadly devoted to him, as the only person in her life who might believe what is happening.

From the kitchen window, Rachel can see far into the woods, back to where the black trunks of the trees blend together into a kind of visual nonsense. Sometimes the trees are wet and full of sun and their naked branches form a brilliant snarl of light. Other days, the snow settles on every twig and the effect is clean and meditative, every surface retraced and made sense of. Rachel knows that there are paths through these woods. Her mother owns the land, but she allows the neighbors to ride their horses through, which brings Rachel a sense of comfort. It somehow makes the whole cold, bitter forest easier to fathom.

I wanted you, she considers saying to Bianca, but she knows how that will sound. A four-year-old will see right through it.

Sometimes, when her mother is not home, Rachel calls Jess. It is not quite loneliness that leads her to this decision, but a kind of suffocating boredom. He could be anyone else at this point, but he just happens to be himself, his miserable, available self.

"How are the sticks?" he asks her every time, and, every time, she regrets her decision to call. The question is somehow repulsive to her, and she is reminded of his long, tolerant face, his slow, mournful desire. She finds herself saying things like "I'm not your girlfriend" and "This is probably the last time I'm ever going to call." She has become catty and spiteful and still full of rangy, insolent lust. When she last spoke to him, about a week ago, he was about to fly out to San Francisco to buy a new guitar. She did not know why he needed to go all the way to San Francisco to buy a guitar and she was annoyed at him for leaving, for seeming so feckless and indulgent. She knew so little about his life—where he got his money, what kept him going in general. He could be moody and immature, and Rachel often feared that she had fallen into a trap, that she had been taken in by a false front, or a secretly volatile personality, and so she was coarse with him, unfair, tyrannical. She had to keep her dignity.

Her mother does not want to know anything about him. No names, no reasons, no confessions, she has always said. I don't want to understand it. But Rachel sometimes worries that her mother carries certain assumptions about Jess, that in her mind, he is nameless, faceless, but somehow still striking and successful, like Rachel's husband. Jess is neither of these things and

Rachel wants credit for it. *Look how low I can stoop,* she wants to say, *how little sense I can make.*

She wants to call him now. She had meant to call him today, before it became clear to her that Bianca would not be going to school. She would like to tell him about the horses in the woods, their magnificent, shadowy procession through her mind; about the horrendous things that children can say. But she has never spoken of Bianca with him. He knows of her existence, of course, but that is all. It is strange to think that there is a part of her life, a lewd, anarchic part, where Bianca does not fit, where no one does.

The girl is back on her feet, doing little hops across the kitchen. Her body is straight and tense, her teeth set in a hard line. Her hair, too, seems to be standing on end, electrified in the dry air. It is wavy and exceptionally blond with streaks so light they are almost white. Strangers often stop her to tell her that she is beautiful. They will ask her, "Do you know that you are beautiful?" And Rachel wonders what they are expecting her to say. Do they hope that she will say, *Yes, yes I know? I have always known?* No. Rachel does not think so. She reaches for Bianca, to brush the hair from her eyes, to trail a finger down her cheek—some idle, motherly gesture that she knows will not help. Bianca stops hopping and holds her arms straight, tightening her fists, locking her knees. Touching her is like touching a wax doll. She has closed herself off. This is her last effort to control her body, to keep everything neatly inside. It must be painful, Rachel thinks, but perhaps not as painful as letting go. She has forgotten that, as a child, she used to do the same thing.

And then when it happens, it happens all in a matter of seconds. Something dawns on Bianca's face, a shocked, ominous look of defeat. She runs from the kitchen and Rachel follows her. She does not hurry—she never hurries after her daughter, unless it is a true emergency—and by the time she catches up to her, Bianca is already in the bathroom, pants around her ankles, looking at the lump on the floor.

Two days before she moved out, Rachel's husband did not wake up at his usual time. Rachel had awoken in Bianca's room, where she had been sleeping on a cot beside the bed. She had explained to Bianca that it was because of Daddy's snoring that she had switched rooms, but it was clear that Bianca was not alarmed. She did not need an explanation for why her mother might want to be closer to her. Rachel went downstairs and made the coffee. She opened the window shades and swept some crumbs from the table into her hand. It was not usual for her to be awake before her husband, and she felt at once a sense of freedom and a terrible responsibility. She could not decide whether her husband's habits were still her concern. It might seem obvious that they wouldn't be, but nothing was obvious anymore. She had expected for a marriage to fall apart, as they are said to, but hers was disappearing gradually, like snow, leaving odd-shaped islands behind—moments of unexpected tenderness, or sudden and vivid memories that had no business appearing when they did. He no longer kissed her in the mornings with his hand on the doorknob, ready to walk out, impatiently, generously. She did not go downstairs to see him after putting Bianca to bed, but stayed at her desk, pretending to read until she was too tired. And yet it seemed that they still made room for each other, emotionally. There was something that Rachel had expected to close in, dramatically, like the entrance to a cave collapsing.

But the cave was still there, with all its chambers, its trafficked areas and its unexplored darknesses. There was still the question of whether or not to wake him. There had always been this question, for he would wake in a confused and angry panic no matter how gentle her tactics. It would be worse, however, to let him be late for work, to stand by while he rushed through breakfast and his shaving, to feel her morning split between his urgency and her guilt. So she went to his room— it had gone from *their* room to *his* room so easily that she wondered if she had always, subconsciously, felt this way—and stood by the bed. It was dark. She could barely make out the pale outline of his cheek above the blanket. What if this is it? she found herself wondering. What if he has died in his sleep? He would have died still married to her, his intentions obliterated. It would be an injustice. She sat at the edge of the mattress and rested her hand on the mound of his shoulder, feeling it rise and fall. She was relieved and sad—sad that they would have to go through with it after all, that she had made him into something that was, for the moment, incomplete. Something stirred beneath the blanket and his hand emerged, touching her lightly in a moment of forgetfulness. A sweet, hopeless error.

◆

"Are you coming?" Bianca calls up the stairs. She has put on her boots and her mittens and is standing in the front hall. Her blond hair, in the light from the doorway, floats around her head in an almost frightful, otherworldly crown.

"Where are we going?" Rachel asks. She is at the top of the stairs. Her hands are full of laundry. She has been putting clothes into a dresser that had once stood in her bedroom as a child. The top coat of red paint is chipped, revealing a dark evergreen underneath. This discovery feels to Rachel like a betrayal of character, the dresser having been one of those solid, immovable staples of childhood.

"The woods, remember?" Bianca puts up her hands, waving her mittens.

Yes. Rachel remembers now. It was one of her many bribes. If you go to the bathroom—if you just sit on the toilet and try—we can go out to lunch, then to the pet store to look at the turtles. We can go for a walk in the woods. Bianca had not shown interest in any of these suggestions, so Rachel had not given them another thought.

"You said there are horses in the woods."

"Sometimes."

"You said we could go."

"Yes." Rachel drops the clothes back into the laundry basket and slides the basket into her room, closing the door so that her mother will not see the chore left undone. This will not stop her mother from opening the door and finding it anyway, but Rachel cannot help herself. She is the type of person who hides candy wrappers and receipts in the trash, photographs between the pages of books. There is a little green dress that she keeps at the back of her closet, for fear that her mother might discover it and know, as if by magic, where it has been.

They have not been in the woods since early fall. Rachel has made many excuses to avoid it: It is too cold, or too late in the day. The snow is too deep, the wind too harsh. But the truth is that she is unnerved by the woods. She feels that time might pass without her knowledge while she is there, or that something will happen that will render her helpless, or hugely inconvenienced. She might lose her contact lenses, or get her socks wet. Some devastation might befall the world and she would not know.

They layer wool socks. They tie scarves under their

coats and fasten the cuffs of their mittens. They do not have any long underwear, so they wear pajamas underneath their pants for warmth. Rachel has written a note for her mother, which she leaves taped to the faucet, where her mother has always left notes so that they will not be missed. They walk outside, squinting at the snow. Bianca trudges ahead with a new determined energy, her body made pudgy and babyish again by her snowsuit. She is shouting happily, some private incoherence that she has not invited Rachel to share, and Rachel wishes that she would be quieter, so that she would not feel so exposed, so rapturously unguarded. "Hush," she says under her breath. She focuses on the fine dusting of snow on the tree trunks, a thread of footprints made by some lightweight animal. She tries to relax.

It has never made sense to her why her mother decided to escape civilization. They had lived in town when Rachel and her brothers were growing up, on a wide, shady street overrun by children on bicycles. Rachel had known all the neighbors' yards intimately— the toolsheds, laundry lines, aboveground swimming pools, all the friendly dogs. The map of her neighborhood was the layout of her freedom. She never needed to go any farther. Later in life she would try to recreate the interiors of the neighbors' houses in her own home, the cool safety of the kitchens, which were conservative and dark in daytime, the tall, blue-carpeted stairways. There were lilac bathrooms and deep, secret bedrooms. The best houses always had a touch of anonymity, she decided, something hotel-like that kept them from becoming too steeped in their own history. When she and her husband bought their first house, she had chosen colors that she had no attachment to—marigold and grays—she filled vases with sprigs of pussy willow, because it seemed sophisticated and did not remind her of any particular season or occasion. Rachel's way of making something hers was to make it plain and bearable.

This is another disadvantage of the woods. Nature has no style, no predictable emotional cues. It is all beautiful and endless. If it stirs anything at all, it stirs something primitive, something beneath nostalgia, or heartache, or love. A tree made into a chair, Rachel thinks, can bring such precise, harmonious longing, but a tree when it is just a tree demands something unbridled, rhapsodic. A crow takes off from a branch above their heads.

"Aw," Bianca says, "it's cute."

There are deer tracks on the trail. The droppings

make little melted nests in the snow, while scattered drops of urine are deep and surgical. Sometimes a clump of snow will float down from the trees and make its own soft mark. Rachel can no longer see the house behind them. She has stopped turning around to look. Her fingers are cold. Her toes have an icy edge.

"Time to turn around now," she calls to Bianca, who has run ahead. The girl stays where she is, facing away, planted stoutly in the snow.

"Bianca." Rachel cups her hands around her mouth, needlessly. It's not as if Bianca cannot hear her. She does not respond, because she is looking at something off the path, deep into the trees: an orange corner of cloth flapping in the wind. It might be a scrap of old tarp, or a jacket left on a branch by one of the fabled riders on horseback. It could be nothing, but to Rachel it is a camp, a fully settled camp in the middle of the forest. She is sure that she can smell it, the foul black odor of a doused campfire, the grimy, lived-in crawl space of the tent. It is not a regular tent with a flexible domed roof, but a makeshift one, an oily canvas draped over a fallen tree and covered by pieces of tarpaulin stitched together with plastic zip ties. The entrance is like a burrow, hollowed out in the snow. It is a black, shabby hole.

How is it that Rachel is aware of this when she cannot possibly see that far? She does not know. She takes Bianca's arm and begins to lead her back along the path toward the house. Her gut is filled with white heat. She is radiant with white, mortal heat, and for once she cannot summon the language to describe what she is doing, or what she is running from. This danger has always existed within her. It has always been possible, just as the bottom of the ocean is possible. Just as the tall, stooped figure has always existed in just that way, with his shoulders peaked and his head lowered, as if gathering himself up to lift a heavy object. He is painted in her mind—a cave drawing, a crude flash of pigment in the back of her thoughts—his image presiding over everything, over every decision that she has ever made. But before he steps out across the path, before he bears himself up in that weary, inevitable way, Rachel thinks of Bianca. She is still looking down at Bianca from the top of the stairs, at the bright static crown of hair flying around her face, her wet petulant mouth, her mittens raised in a bold salute, and she thinks, Not now. Not yet.

Acknowledgments

Many of these stories have appeared in other publications: "Something for a Young Woman" in *New England Review* (2015), later reprinted in *The O. Henry Prize Stories 2017* and *Literary Hub*; "Arla Had Horses" in *West Branch* (2017); "Single" in *Post Road* (2020); "Rodeo" in *The Massachusetts Review* (2016); "Trespassers" in *New England Review* (2016); "If *Tooth* Could Mean Heart" in *Arts & Letters* (2019); "Schematic" in *Willow Springs* (2016); "Gorgon" in *JuxtaProse* (2019); and "Prepare Her" in *The Southern Review* (2019), later excerpted in *Literary Hub*.

To my agent, Reiko Davis, and my editor, Leigh Newman. You gave me what I needed most when I needed it. We also happened to put a book into the world. Thank you both. You have no idea.

Thanks to my professors, especially Annabel Davis-Goff, April Bernard, Marguerite Feitlowitz, and Mark

ACKNOWLEDGMENTS

Wunderlich, who taught me how to read so I could teach myself to write.

To my friends, Anne, Keenan, Rebekah, Douglas, Gabriele, and Andrew: Thank you for wading through the sludge of my first stories. They are better now because of you.

Thanks to all the editors of the literary magazines who supported me, especially Carolyn Kuebler, from *New England Review*. It has been a thrill working with you and reading your beautiful publications.

Megan Mayhew Bergman, Lori Ostlund, and Anne Raeff: You have been such an inspiration. Thank you for answering all my questions over the years.

Thank you, Meg H., for listening and for being proud of me.

To my parents: I love you.

And thanks to my loving family, to Ava and Frances and Wilson. To Jackson and Lucas, for making my world better.

To Jamie: everything.

GENEVIEVE PLUNKETT
is the recipient of an O. Henry Award. Her work has also appeared in *The Best Small Fictions* and journals such as *New England Review, The Southern Review, Crazyhorse, Colorado Review,* and *Willow Springs*. She lives in Vermont with her two children.